"You have nothing to fear from me, Martha."

"Really? You are holding me against my will and yet you say I have nothing to fear? Were I to scream, my father and all our neighbors would be out here in a heartbeat ready to lynch you from the nearest tree."

"Then scream if you're truly afraid."

She hesitated and his heart stopped.

At last she let out a defeated sigh. "Fine. I won't scream."

His arms ached, more from wrestling earlier with the upturned wagon than from holding her small, warm body. "Promise me you won't run away and I'll let you down."

She nodded.

He couldn't hold her all night, as much as he wanted to, so he lowered her to her feet, keeping one arm around her waist. She stood against him, her hands resting on his chest. Had she forgotten, or did she want them there?

D1239460

Books by Davalynn Spencer

Love Inspired Heartsong Presents

The Rancher's Second Chance
The Cowboy Takes a Wife
Branding the Wrangler's Heart
Romancing the Widow

DAVALYNN SPENCER's

love of writing has taken her from the city crime beat and national rodeo circuit to college classrooms and inspirational publication. When not writing Western romance or teaching, she speaks at women's retreats and plays on her church's worship team. She and her husband have three children and four grandchildren and make their home on Colorado's Front Range with a Queensland heeler named Blue. To learn more about Davalynn visit her website at www.davalynnspencer.com.

DAVALYNN SPENCER

Romancing the Widow

HEARTSONG
PRESENTS

Recycling programs
for this product may
not exist in your area.

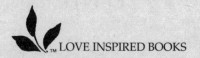

™ LOVE INSPIRED BOOKS

ISBN-13: 978-0-373-48721-9

ROMANCING THE WIDOW

www.Harlequin.com

Printed in U.S.A.

Now faith is the substance of things hoped for,
the evidence of things not seen.
—*Hebrews* 11:1

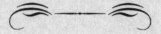

For all who hope in God's unfailing love.

Chapter 1

Colorado 1888

Martha Mae Stanton yanked the satin ribbon beneath her chin and jerked off the ridiculous black hat. Digging her nails into the fine netting, she ripped the veil away and tossed it on the seat beside her.

A long, hot train ride was one thing. Making that ride while behind a socially dictated curtain was quite another.

Across the aisle, a matron gasped and clutched her reticule to her bulging bosom. Martha picked up the veil, leaned into the narrow walkway and dropped the netting on the woman's shelflike lap. "Here. You wear it. I've had enough."

The matron sputtered and huffed and swatted the black tulle from her knees as if it were a stinging hornet.

A smile almost made it to Martha's dry lips but died for lack of sustenance.

She leaned back against the plush green seat and squeezed her eyes shut. The late afternoon sun boiled through her window. Grit dusted her teeth, and perspiration gathered beneath her arms and dribbled down her back. September had never been so sticky—not in the Rocky Mountains.

Mimicking the matron a half hour later, the Denver & Rio Grande wheezed to a coughing stop at Cañon City's depot. Steam hissed along the wheels and a knot tightened in Martha's neck. She retied the hat as impatient travelers rushed the aisle. Weary mothers herded their petulant young ahead of them, reminding Martha of her former students—and the children she would never bear.

The porter stopped at her seat with a shining smile and a tip of his cap. "This be your stop, ma'am. Last one today."

"Yes—yes, I know." She looked toward the open door at the end of the car, caught the shouts of reuniting families. With a deep breath she stood and gripped the seat back ahead of her, giving her legs a moment to remember how to proceed.

"May I carry that for you, ma'am?" He reached for her bag.

"No. Thank you." She curled her fingers into the handle, desperate for something to ground her, keep her from running back down the rails.

She made her way to the exit and paused at the step, scanning the crowd for her parents. They stood apart, the only two people not huddled with arriving passengers. A smiling mask lay hard against her mother's gentle face. Martha recognized it from the countless times her father had dealt with the more unpleasant duties of his calling.

She should not have returned. Regret slid from the back of her damp collar and pooled at her waist. She did not want her family to see her as an unpleasant obligation.

The porter cleared his throat. "You all right, ma'am?"

She plucked at her high collar. "I'm fine. Thank you."

Breathing in a dusty draught, she descended to the step and then the ground. Her father appeared and drew her into his arms. Silent. Strong. He held her close, knowing as always exactly what to do.

Her mother wrapped an arm around each of them and bent her lilac-scented hair toward Martha. The fragrance embraced her as closely as her parents and drew her back through the years.

"I am so sorry." Her mother's whisper fell as gently as her scent.

Martha pulled from the embrace and met troubled eyes—her father's black as her mourning dress but shining with love. Her mother's, burnished and beautiful as ever, though age had etched their corners.

"Thank you," Martha said. "Both of you. Let's go home."

It was a short walk to the buggy, and she and her mother climbed in while the porter helped her father strap her trunk to the back. Settling her carpetbag at her feet, Martha glanced toward the depot's long covered platform. In a shadowed corner, an abutment jutted from the building and a man leaned against it. Had the sun not been at a sharp angle, she would have missed him in his dark clothing, hat pulled just below the level of his eyes. One knee bent with the booted foot resting on the wall. His thumbs hooked his trousers, draping back a black coat.

It was too hot for a coat of any kind.

She didn't realize she was staring until he raised his head a hairbreadth and bore into her with a blue gaze.

Steeled, perhaps by months of grief, she held his scrutiny without reaction, measuring him as he measured her. Lean and alone, like a wolf. So unlike her beloved Joseph.

All black, like her widow's weeds.

Her jaw clenched at the phrase, and the tightness coupled like a freight car to her cramping neck. It was bad enough to be shrouded in spirit, bereft and singular after sharing life with a fine and caring man. Her eyes pinched at the corners, dry and tearless. Depleted.

She looked down at her pale hands, as white as Joseph's still face, clutched against the gloomy skirt. The memory seared through her chest, scorching what little vibrancy remained. All her hopes and promise of a future lay buried in a pine coffin.

Her father climbed into the seat, gathered the reins and tapped old Dolly's rump.

A shudder rippled through Martha. Cramped as they were, her mother leaned even closer with concern. "Are you ill, Marti?"

The old nickname rang foreign in Martha's ears. No one had called her Marti since she'd graduated and married Joseph three years ago. She glanced over her shoulder as if the name belonged to someone else. The stranger's eyes caught hers.

Foolishness flooded her cheeks, a convincing sign for her mother to think she was feverish.

"No, Mama, I'm fine. Just—just noticing all the changes in Cañon City." A flimsy excuse, one sure to wither beneath her mother's scalding scrutiny. But the woman had pity on her only daughter and simply patted Martha's folded hands.

"Yes, a lot has changed since last you were here."

Everyone looked the same to Haskell Tillman Jacobs—road-weary, dusty and glad to be off the train. Everyone but the red-haired beauty in black.

Anonymity suited him and he preferred to blend in with whatever background availed itself. But she had stared straight at him as if she knew the man he sought and could tell him the varmint's whereabouts.

Obscurity returned when the parson drove them from the depot and turned east onto Main Street toward home at the opposite end. Knowing what people did and where they lived was part of Haskell's job.

He just hadn't known about *her*.

He pushed from the wall, left the wooden platform and

stopped at the second car. The porter leaned down for the step. Haskell pulled back one side of his coat.

The man straightened. "Yes, sir?"

"Anyone else on the train?"

"No, sir. This our last stop."

"I'd like to see for myself."

The porter stepped aside. "Yes, sir."

The interior smelled of sweaty clothing, dust and sour lunches. Haskell walked the narrow aisle, scanned the seats for any telltale sign or forgotten belonging. The porter followed.

"There ain't nothin' left behind, sir. I done checked it all."

Haskell cast a look at the man who obviously took his job as seriously as Haskell took his, but continued on, pausing at each bench.

Something lay on the floor halfway back. He bent to look beneath the seat, snatched the dark netting and wadded it into his vest pocket. He opened the door, passed through to the next car and repeated his inspection. At the opposite end, he turned to his dogged follower.

"And a fine job you've done."

"You lookin' for somethin' special?"

The man's voice carried more than the cursory question. He saw more than most.

"Where did the woman in black board the train?"

"You mean the widow Stanton? Kansas City, sir."

Haskell fingered the netting.

"You pick up anyone in Pueblo today?"

"Just a mother and her two young'uns. If'n somebody else jumped on the back, I couldn't say." Coal-black eyes looked to the low ceiling. "We carried a body or two without knowin' it at the time." He regarded Haskell with a near smile. "But not in a *long* time." His thick brown fingers flexed open and closed.

Haskell nodded and stepped outside. "I'll have a look."

When the train had arrived, he'd seen no movement on top of the cars, saw no one jump. At least not on the depot side.

Climbing up, he scanned the length of the train and found what he expected—nothing. He squinted back along the rail bed, noted the houses huddled near the track with small fenced yards hedging the narrow road between the gravel bed and their gates.

Working his way down, he jumped clear and walked downtown.

Word had it that the man he sought was last seen in La Junta and headed this way by train. Obviously, the speed and comfort of such travel balanced out the risk, especially for one so gifted at slipping into a crowd unseen.

He could have missed him once the widow stepped down. She'd drawn Haskell's eye like a prospector's nose to a nugget. The hazards of a solitary life, he figured. But he had no intention of being turned from his purpose.

He pulled the black netting from his vest pocket. Intricate needlework hung from one side, stretched and torn thread from the other. Crumpling the ripped piece, he dropped it in a wire basket just inside the front doors of the Hotel St. Cloud.

Across the lobby, the dining room beckoned and he took his usual table in the farthest corner. A seat against the wall offered a clear view of the guests who dotted the room. He set his hat in an empty chair.

The Yale University professor with more hair on his face than his head dined with his entourage, each member intent upon impressing the easterner with some tidbit of knowledge.

The serving girl interrupted Haskell's observation with her coffee and inviting smile.

"Good evening, Mr. Tillman." She righted the cup on his saucer and filled it to just beneath the brim.

"Evening. Thank you."

"Did you enjoy your day?"

She waited expectantly for him to answer, but he didn't chitchat with girls young enough to be his daughter and obviously angling for a beau.

"Yes. And what's on the board tonight?"

The smile slid away and she pulled the coffeepot to her waist. "Roast beef, mashed potatoes with gravy, green beans and peach pie. Will you be dining alone again?"

She didn't give up easily, he'd give her that.

"Yes." He reached for the coffee without looking up.

She huffed away in a swirl of skirts and stopped at the Bentons' table, her smile back in place, her coffee at the ready.

If the food wasn't so good, he'd eat his fill of canned peaches and jerky in his room. But it wasn't often he found fare like the new hotel offered. Cañon City had more to recommend it than its bathhouse and hanging train bridge in the canyon.

Which were a few of the reasons he'd considered sticking around, maybe settling down.

The young widow's bold gaze rose before him, framed by her black hat and coppery hair.

Her image nettled him. Irritated him. He had business to attend to and could not be distracted by a beautiful, aloof woman.

"I tell you, the second quarry will be as forthcoming as the first."

Drawn by the professor's insistent tone, Haskell tuned his ear to the conversation at the far wall. An animated man, the easterner waved his fork like a bandleader's baton.

"Finch has made further discovery across the gully and has been digging there for several weeks now with great success."

The listeners murmured over their plates, and from the gleam of fortune in the speaker's eye, Haskell guessed the man and his absentee companion—Finch—had uncovered an oil bed or a rich ore vein.

"I am confident that these bones will rival even the Allosaurus and Diplodocus unearthed here a decade ago. Perhaps another Stegosaurus will be discovered, even more complete than the first."

Haskell coughed as the hot coffee slid down his windpipe. He set the china cup in its saucer and wiped his mouth on the linen napkin.

If he recalled his school days accurately, the bald professor in the fine jacket was talking about dinosaurs.

Chapter 2

Martha stood in the doorway and looked around her old room—that of a girl on her way to college. She set her bag on the trunk her father had placed at the foot of the iron bed and flopped onto the bright, fan-patterned quilt. Running her fingers along the fine stitches, she recalled the piercing needle that had bit repeatedly until she got the feel of the thimble.

She removed her hat and tossed the dreary thing aside. With a heavy sigh she hugged a pink pillow to her chest and fell back across the bed.

Life had not turned out as she'd hoped.

Familiar footsteps sounded on the stairs, but Martha had no energy to sit up and invite her mother in. Nor had she the right. This was no longer her home, though she had called it such at the station.

She turned her head toward the door.

"Supper's in a half hour. Will you be down?"

"Perhaps."

Her mother came in and sat on the bed. "There is a new seamstress in town. We can visit her in the next few days and pick out some lighter fabric for a new dress or two."

Martha huffed. "You don't like my widow's weeds?"

"No, I do not."

Such characteristic honesty did not surprise Martha, but it bolstered her enough to sit up.

"It's been more than a year, Marti. You are young and

beautiful and smart, and it breaks my heart to see you grieving away to nothing." She pulled one of Martha's hands from the pillow and pressed her fingers. "Life goes on—like the river. Ever the same but with new water fresh from the mountains."

Martha turned her hand over and closed her fingers around her mother's. "It's hard, Mama. It's not only that I miss Joseph so much, I just don't know *how* to go on living."

Her mother nodded but said nothing.

"I buried my heart with him." The whisper fell so lightly Martha doubted it had been heard.

An aching smile pulled her mother's lips. "I know, dear. Not exactly how you feel at losing your husband, but I know how it feels to lose someone you love. That person leaves an irreplaceable hole in your heart—like your grandfather did in mine." She tightened her fingers. "But we go on in Christ's strength. He shares our sorrow. He grieved when His friend Lazarus died."

Martha pulled her hand free. "But Jesus brought Lazarus back. He hasn't brought back Grandpa or Joseph, and Joseph was a minister. A preacher, like Daddy, who loved his wife and his congregation. A man who should not have been struck down by a stray bullet in a street brawl."

Anger stiffened Martha's aching neck and her fists clenched involuntarily. Her mother stood and faced her.

"I could not agree more. Life is not fair. But it is life. While you are home with us, I pray you will take it up again." She leaned forward and lightly kissed Martha's forehead. "Come down when you are ready. We'll be waiting."

Martha let out a deep sigh and surveyed the bookshelf her father had built when she was in grammar school. A china-faced doll sat on top in her beautiful blue taffeta dress. Below, an assortment of rocks and fossil fragments remained where Martha had left them beside a stack of books on paleontology.

At one time she had fancied herself a pioneer in the male-dominated field. Her enthusiastic pursuit had earned her a seat at Michigan's Albion College, where Joseph studied. How quickly his kind nature had turned her interest from things long dead to the handsome seminary student so full of life. She had gladly laid aside her earlier passion to be his wife.

And now he lay beneath the same earth that had hidden her once-cherished fossils.

The irony bit into her with a carnivorous crunch.

She replaced the pillow against the headboard and slapped her hands against her lap. Dust blossomed from her skirt and powdered her palms. She removed her short jacket and hung it over the footboard to beat outside tomorrow with her skirt. Her shirtwaist would do for an evening at home.

Time allowed a quick scrub of her hands and face before joining her parents at the table. The tepid water in the pitcher woke her from her doldrums, and the lavender oil refreshed her in a way she'd forgotten.

Food did not appeal to her, but a cup of tea might soothe her stomach and her spirit.

She unpacked her satchel, loosened her hair and let it fall unhindered. With the porcelain-backed brush and comb set Joseph had given her on their wedding night, she smoothed the knots and tangles until her fingers pulled smoothly through the length. Then she plaited it into a long rope and secured the end with a ribbon. Joseph had liked her to wear her hair down rather than up in the style of the day, and it had been her delight to please him.

Placing the matching set on her dressing table, she looked in the glass and saw her mother from twenty years before. At least Martha knew how she would look someday. But aging as gracefully as her mother in manner as well as appearance was far beyond Martha's capabilities.

Downstairs, she paused at the kitchen doorway. Her parents still ate there rather than in the formal dining room, and when she entered, her father stood and offered his hand. Martha took it and allowed him to draw her into a brief embrace. She kissed his cheek and took the chair she hadn't claimed in seven years.

Such a short time. And yet it felt like a lifetime.

The plates already held corn bread and sliced ham, and her mother brought coffee to the table as well as a pot of tea.

"I thought you might prefer tea this evening," she said as she placed each vessel on a hot pad.

"Thank you, Mama. You were right." Martha pulled the old silver sugar bowl from the table's center and spooned in a helping, then poured the aromatic brew. She set the pot on its thick cloth, laid a hand in her father's upturned palm, the other in her mother's and bowed her head.

"Thank You, Lord, for bringing Marti safely to us," her father said. "Comfort her, Lord. Heal her with Your love, in Your timing. Amen."

Her father never had been one to preach a sermon in his prayers, and for that she had always been grateful. But he, too, used her informal name—the moniker that had stuck until she enrolled at Albion.

She may have come home, but she could never come back and be who she once was.

The warm corn muffin broke apart in her hands and she buttered half. "So who's minding the mercantile now?"

A look shot between her parents like lightning across the sky. She took a bite and waited for what must be bad news. Had they sold it since Grandpa Whitaker's passing two years before?

Her mother held a napkin to her lips then picked up her coffee. "We wanted to talk to you about that."

Martha laid the muffin in her plate. Talk to her? About the mercantile? "Did you sell it?"

"I couldn't. Can't." Her mother's brows pulled together over pained eyes. "Foolish, I know, but I can't let it go. It's outdated and old-fashioned and other modern stores outshine it. But the mercantile is what brought Daddy and me here, what introduced me to your father—that and Dolly." She reached for his hand and he caught hers with a warm smile that tightened Martha's chest.

"We wondered if you might be interested in running the store." He idly stroked her mother's hand with his thumb. "Just for a while, until we find someone to run it full-time."

The suggestion made Martha's head hurt. She hadn't been required to make a decision since the deacons told her they would take care of all the funeral arrangements and asked her to choose a headstone. The reasoning part of her brain didn't work, and she rubbed her right temple, hoping to prod the lax organ into action.

"I—I don't know."

"You don't have to answer now." Her mother warmed her tea. "We had not intended to spring it on you so suddenly. Take your time and think it over. Your grandmother still works every morning, and a young man is helping in the afternoon until we find someone more permanent. We just thought—"

"You just thought it would be good for me." Martha regretted the steel that edged her voice, but they were doing it again. And she a grown woman now. They had sent her away to school to protect her—they said—from Tad Overton. They had suggested she become a teacher—they said—because she had such a way with the children at church. And now they had planned the rest of her life here in Cañon City, tucked safely behind the counter of Whitaker's Mercantile.

"If you'll excuse me, I'm rather tired from my trip." She took her plate to the sink and scraped her meal into the chicken scrap tin. When she turned around, her mother and father still held each other's hands. Her mother's head dipped forward, hiding her expression.

"We'll see you in the morning, Marti." Her father offered a loving smile. "Sleep well."

Aching with regret and frustration and anger, she dashed up the staircase and slammed her door with the intensity of her childhood.

More shame.

She leaned against the door and slid to the floor. At last the tears came, burning and purging, like great stinging drops of acid.

Haskell stood at the east window of his third-floor room watching dawn crest the Main Street buildings. Within a month the sun would slide south along the horizon and rise a half hour later.

But his internal clock woke him at the same time every morning, summer and winter. Something he had learned from his father.

He'd paid extra for the corner room, well worth it for the view of the depot a few blocks to the east. Steam rose from the train's stack as it coughed and cleared its throat, preparing to pull through the narrow gorge, up the grade and on to Leadville.

He rubbed his face and ran both hands through his hair. One more day and he'd visit the barber. But today he'd walk the road that hugged the south side of the tracks. Keep an eye out for any last-minute passengers hopping a car.

He grabbed his hat and locked the door behind him.

Few people were on the streets at this hour, but enough

to garner his scrutiny. Merchants, bankers—those he'd seen before. No new faces. He cut down a side street and crossed the tracks east of the depot. Lights shone from the row houses fronting the narrow road, and ribbons of frying bacon laced the morning. His stomach growled and an old yearning stirred.

Food wasn't all he longed for, but a warm smile and a loving woman to come home to. A family, maybe a few acres of his own outside of town. The law was a mean-spirited mistress and had kept him on the move for too long. It was time.

The widow's face flashed before him, sober, pale, bold. Not exactly what he had in mind for a wife. But her image dogged him and he couldn't shake free of her. Even in his dreams she stared, peeling away his veneer as easily as skinning a spud.

Who was she—other than the parson's widowed daughter come home to mourn? That much he'd overheard in the hotel parlor last night after supper. But *who* was she? *What* was she that she stuck in his mind like a burr to a saddle blanket?

He shook his head and cleared it enough to focus on the empty street that stretched ahead. A cottonwood stood halfway between the houses and the depot, and he took up his post on its west side with a clear view of both. If any man crossed over, he'd see him. And if the man jumped the cars without benefit of a ticket, Haskell would be obliged to help him detrain.

He pulled his watch from his vest pocket, ran his thumb over the engraved *TJ* and flipped open the cover. The train whistle blew and the watch face read five minutes to six. Right on time. He slid the timepiece in its shallow pocket and reset his hat. If his quarry were here, he'd be showing himself any minute.

The tree's rough bark bit through his coat sleeve by the

time the train had built up a full head of steam and eased out of the station. No one stole from the houses across the tracks. No one dodged out at the last minute to swing onto the back of a car.

Haskell pushed off the tree and rubbed his arm. Maybe his information was wrong. Crossing the tracks, he headed for the telegraph office.

The sleepy-eyed operator opened the door, clearly displeased at being asked to send a telegram so early. Haskell penned a coded message, signed the agreed-upon alias and pushed the paper across the counter. "Send it to Captain Teller Blain, Colorado Rangers, Denver."

He followed the paper with two bits and answered the operator's curious regard with a cold stare. "You can reach me at the St. Cloud."

Haskell reset his hat and walked toward the hotel. He'd eaten there twice a day for the last five and though it was good, he needed a change. Smoke curled from a mercantile chimney in the next block. He crossed the street and stopped before the door, held open by a flatiron. The front windows were filled with the usual wares—stoves, dishes, barrels and sacks of provisions. Toward the back two men sat in front of a potbellied stove. Much too warm for that sort of thing.

An older woman poured coffee from a blue-speckled pot and saw him as she lifted her head. Her hand beckoned and out of respect he removed his hat and stepped inside.

The aroma of fresh biscuits lured him to join the other hapless prey by the stove. If the panfry lived up to its smell, it'd be worth sitting so close to a fire on a clear September morning.

Shadowed at the back of the store another woman worked at a long counter. A thick braid hung to apron strings tied at her waist. The hair's color registered a warning, but she turned before he took notice. Her dark eyes

locked on him and held him to the worn wooden floor. She
halted but showed no expression. Her porcelain skin did
not pink as did that of the young waitress at the hotel. In a
breath she collected herself and continued forward, bearing two plates of biscuits floating in molasses. She gave
one to each man without so much as a word.

"And you must be hungry yourself, young man."

He turned to the diminutive white-haired woman who
wore a bright smile and offered him a tin cup filled with
coffee. Few people called him young anymore, but she had
the right, judging by her snowy crown.

"Thank you, ma'am." He took the remaining empty
chair and acknowledged the other two men as briefly as
possible.

Without her black suit and hat, and with her auburn hair
hanging down her back, the widow appeared younger than
she had at the train station. Softer. But not in her countenance. It remained stony and unresponsive as she handed
him a blue tin plate with two biscuits and molasses.

"Thank you."

Her eyes skimmed past his before focusing beyond his
shoulder.

"You are welcome."

Did he imagine it or hear it? Her voice was a wind whisper in tall pines, a sigh of evening breeze across prairie
grass. It chilled him and warmed him at the same time.

He stared at his plate, telling himself to use the fork
that lay across it.

The others ate as if they were about to be hanged. He
set his cup on the floor and balanced the deep-lipped plate
on one leg.

The first bite threw the St. Cloud's heavy bread into
disgrace. The second pulled his heart up through his gullet, and the third finished the biscuit. The word fell short

of describing the fare, as far short as red told the color of the widow's braid.

Without watching her, he followed her movements, felt the shifting air as she passed, smelled the faintest lavender when she reached for his empty plate.

Again the voice, stronger this time. Purer. "Do you care for more?"

He looked at her hands, avoided her eyes, for they would make a beggar of him, ranger or no.

Shaking his head, he handed her the plate. "But thank you." The hot tin cup offered distraction, and he gripped it, drawing the coffee's burn through his fingers.

The other men left, the older woman filled his cup again and time stood still. The fire died, his brow cooled and he remembered what he was about.

He raised his head to find the widow gone. Scanning the room, his gaze rested on a closed doorway at the back. Abruptly he stood, clapped on his hat and set the cup on the cold stove. At the counter he laid his money down and thanked the older woman.

"She makes the best, don't you agree?" Her pleasant voice broke through his clouded state.

Ignoring his silence, she continued. "Marti. She makes the best biscuits in these Rocky Mountains. Just like her mother, Annie, did years ago." She opened the till and dropped in the coins. "Drew me in, I tell you. That and her handsome grandfather, God rest his soul. But Marti's got her mother's touch, that's for sure."

The matron sent him off with a cherubic smile. "You come back, now."

He touched the brim of his hat and made for the open door and fresh air. Had he dreamed it all or had he just spent the morning in an old mercantile, mesmerized by a beautiful young woman?

The sun's position agreed with his pocket watch.

He turned toward the livery at the end of town. A hard ride would do him good. He'd scour the river, search for cold campfires, maybe find what he was looking for. Get his wits about him.

Chapter 3

Martha ran down the alley behind the Main Street stores until she came to the livery. Leaning against the old gray barn, she gathered her breath and her composure. The dark stranger unsettled her and it had cost her every ounce of her shaky strength to conceal the fact. Her legs trembled from the brief sprint, and her pulse hammered in her temples. She'd never felt so poorly. A year of inactivity, other than teaching, had weakened her, left her vulnerable. No horseback riding, no long walks, no working in a garden since Joseph had died, and now she felt she might follow him at any moment.

She pressed her back against the rough boards and drew in long, deep breaths. She surely *would* die if she didn't find something to do with herself. But working in the mercantile was not the answer. Not with men like…like…disarming strangers who could be outlaws or gunslingers or ne'er-do-wells of any sort.

Twice she had seen him in as many days, and both times he'd affected her the same way, making her shamefully curious about a man other than her beloved Joseph.

She rubbed her hands down her skirt front, annoyed to see the apron. It must be returned, but not now. Not today. She loosened the strings, folded the white cloth and rolled it into a bundle. If her mother hadn't insisted she go to the mercantile…

She stomped her foot. Oh—it was happening again.

People telling her what to do and how to do it. She'd not be a storekeeper, not even temporarily.

The thought of her grandmother's cheerful countenance flooded Martha with remorse. How could she, the woman's namesake, *not* help?

Deflated by an inbred sense of duty, Martha twisted the apron as if wringing water from laundry and walked up the alley between the livery corral and the boot maker's. She'd return the apron tomorrow.

At Main Street, she watched a passing buckboard with laughing children jostling in the back. A man and woman sat on the bench and they pulled up in front of the mercantile. The woman turned to the youngsters, and even from a distance her ultimatum was clear. The squirming bunch quieted and stilled and nodded their blond heads.

Joseph was blond. His children might have looked like that, if she had been able to bear them. Her mind's eye filled with the doctor's shaking head and deathlike pronouncement.

Clutching the rolled apron, Martha stepped into the street. The sudden scramble of iron-shod hooves, a man's shout and a horse's breathy snort were the last she heard before slamming into the hard-packed road with her head.

The ground pushed hard against her, gritty and gouged with ruts. Her dress must be ruined. She turned her head to the side, tried to inhale, but her chest refused the air. Panic licked her spine.

Where was the apron? Why was she lying in the road? She tried to sit up, but pain shot through her ribs and shoulder.

"Can you hear me?"

Piercing blue eyes stared down at her from beneath a dark and frowning brow.

"Blink once if you can hear me." The voice was as deep as the blue pools.

She blinked or, rather, closed her eyes. When she opened them, the face was still there, but closer. So close she could see the lavender rim circling blue irises and smell coffee on the lips beneath them.

"Can you move?"

She made to sit up again but fell back at the sharp stab in her right shoulder.

Another man appeared above her, the blacksmith from the looks of his soiled leather apron. "She's the parson's daughter. They live behind the church across the way."

Impatience rolled through the blue gaze and their owner straightened. "I know." He spoke to the smithy. "Tie my horse to the rail. I'll be back."

The man leaned in again, his features softening. "I'm Haskell Jacobs. I'm going to pick you up, get you off the street and to your home. Blink once if you understand."

She blinked.

He slid one arm beneath her shoulder, cringing when she flinched. The other arm slipped beneath her knees and he lifted her as he stood. She closed her eyes and fought the nausea that roiled in her stomach.

O Lord, the very man I feared has me in his arms and I am helpless! Forcing her eyes open she tried to guess his intended destination. He crossed the street and took the lane beside her father's church. At least he was headed in the right direction.

Against her will her eyes closed and her churning stomach threatened to expose everything she had eaten that morning. She gritted her teeth, but the nausea increased. Her left arm was pinned against a hard chest and her right lay across her lap. She wiggled her fingers and raised her hand to her face, wincing at the effort.

"Don't try to move."

The deep voice rumbled against her ear. Gruff, yet

gentle, as much a paradox as flashing eyes beneath a black scowl.

She fingered her temple and found gravel and dampness.

"You hit hard. You're bleeding, but you need not be frightened. I've got you now."

She looked up as he spoke and caught the comfort he offered in spite of his looks.

"Marti!"

Her mother's cry startled her and pain shot through her shoulder again. Closing her eyes, she turned her face against the stranger's chest. A man's smell filled her senses—warmth, sweat, an equine earthiness. His heart pounded as hard and fast as the horse's hooves had danced around her. *His* horse's hooves? He had nearly run her down and now he was carrying her up the porch steps.

"Is she all right?" Fear rippled her mother's voice as she held the door open to the parlor. The stranger—Haskell?— set her gently on the settee and tucked a cushion behind her neck before pulling his arm away.

"Do you have a doctor in Cañon City?" he asked her mother.

"Yes. Doc Mason's place is at the other end of town."

"I'll ride down and get him. It's the least I can do."

Martha fought against her heavy eyes to catch her mother's expression.

"What do you mean? What happened?"

"She stepped in front of my horse at the livery. When he reared, a front leg knocked her to the ground. She may have broken her shoulder." He touched his hat brim and backed toward the door. "I'd best be getting the doctor, ma'am. My apologies. I'll cover any expenses."

The front door closed and Martha's consciousness threatened to do the same. Her mother's skirts whis-

pered near and Martha forced her eyes open again. Worry
pinched her mother's brow.

Martha raised her left hand toward her mother who
caught it. Her eyes refused to focus and fluttered closed.

A warm hand brushed across her forehead. "I'll be right
back. I'm going to get a cool cloth and clean you up a bit."

Martha tried to nod, but the effort added to her nausea.
She heaved a sigh and sank into the cushion.

Haskell heeled Cache into a lope and kept a careful eye
on the boardwalk and cross streets for anyone who might
rush in front of him. He didn't need to run down another
careless pedestrian.

What was she thinking, charging out that way? Did the
widow have a death wish?

She'd caught him off guard at every turn, and as she'd
lain ashen and unmoving in the street, death was what
he feared. The gash on her head had stopped his heart.
Stopped the very blood in his veins. Thank God, she lived.

He hadn't thanked God for anything in a long time.

He reined in at a yellow, two-story house with green
shutters. A sign hung from the porch: *Marion Mason,
M.D., Surgeon, Dentist.*

Dismounting, he looped the reins over a fence picket.
At the covered porch, he knocked on a door marked *Surgery* and stepped inside.

"Hello?" He took off his hat.

A worn-looking woman came from an adjoining room,
wiping her hands on a white bloodstained towel. "You
need help?"

He'd never met a woman doctor. "You Doc Mason?"

Her thin brows wrenched together. "No. He's washing
up. Give him a minute and he'll see you." She gestured to
a row of mismatched chairs against the front wall. "Have
a seat."

He remained standing.

"Suit yourself."

Her manner, not her gender, made him glad she wasn't the doctor.

She returned to the surgery and muffled voices blended above a groan. Haskell made out the word *laudanum* and watched the doorway. Feet scuffed on the hardwood, a chair scraped across the floor.

He glanced outside at Cache, still wide-eyed and nervous after the collision, ears swiveling at every street noise. The dark gray sidled up along the fence to keep one eye on the road.

Haskell huffed. Even his horse knew better than to have his back to the door.

At a clearing throat, Haskell spun, caught less prepared than his horse.

"May I help you?" A balding man with wire-rim glasses halfway down his nose and shirtsleeves rolled halfway up his arms walked to the center of the room and waited. His hands were ruddy from a recent scrubbing. The scent of alcohol wrapped his short stature.

"A woman's been hurt. She's the parson's daughter. Can you come and look at her?"

The doctor rolled down his cuffs as he returned Haskell's query with one of his own. "Which parson? There is more than one, you know."

Haskell clenched his jaw. He couldn't keep his thoughts clear when the widow had them in an uproar. "At the other end of town, behind the white clapboard church. She's a widow. The daughter, I mean."

The doctor perked up. "Marti Hutton—er, Stanton? Pastor and Annie Hutton's daughter? What happened?"

Haskell's jaw cramped tighter. He didn't need questions, he needed action. "She was knocked to the ground by a horse. Stepped into the street without looking."

"I'll get my bag and meet you there. My buggy's out back." With that, the doctor left Haskell standing in the parlor like a dismissed child. A back door closed hard and he took that as his cue to leave. Shoving his hat on, he crossed the short yard, lifted Cache's reins from the picket and swung up.

So much for a ride along the river.

At the livery he pulled off Cache's rig and carried it inside where hammer pings rang from the back of the barn.

Pete Schultz wasted no daylight. Every door and window was fastened open and a draft pulled through the alleyway, sweeping the furnace heat from the stable.

Haskell stowed his tack and returned to the parsonage behind the church. A buggy waited in front of the house with a sleepy-eyed nag in the harness. Doc Mason's.

Covering the three steps in one leap, he paused at the screen door.

"Yes, he brought her in just moments ago, then rode to fetch you," said Mrs. Hutton.

Being the subject of a woman's conversation wasn't the most comfortable thing he'd endured, especially since the accident was his fault.

Check that. It was *not* his fault.

He knocked on the door frame.

Mrs. Hutton pushed open the screen. "Come in. The doctor's just arrived."

He snatched his hat. It'd been in his hands more than on his head that day.

Doc Mason sat on a low stool pulled close to Marti—or Mrs. Stanton or Ms. Hutton. What did a man call a widow, especially one as young and striking as this one?

The blue velvet settee set off her copper hair as if designed to do just that.

Mason leaned close to the widow's ear and gentled his voice. "Can you tell me exactly what happened?"

Haskell cleared his throat. "I can."

The doctor turned and glowered over his wire frames. "Well, speak up."

"She stepped in front of my horse."

Expressionless, the doctor continued to stare. "And?"

"He reared and when he came down, his knee knocked her to the ground."

"Didn't you see her coming?"

I was distracted. Haskell stiffened. He didn't have to answer to this man, or anyone. "She hit hard."

His eyes flicked to the purple swelling beneath the now-clean gash. "May have broken her shoulder."

Mason turned back to his patient and held his hand against her brow. An odd resentment prodded Haskell.

"Come over here and help Mrs. Hutton. I'm going to palpate Marti's shoulder and you need to hold her still."

Annie Hutton's eyes locked on Haskell's as if daring him to harm her daughter again. A she-bear ready to charge. He laid his hat beneath a chair and took his place at the widow's feet. He'd set his share of bones, but out on the trail, not in a parson's parlor. And they'd been men's bones, not those of a fragile young woman with a worried mother at hand. Just to be safe he pulled the widow's skirt hem over the buttoned shoes, then wrapped both hands around ankles he could snap with a flick of his wrist.

Mrs. Hutton placed a hand on her daughter's left shoulder and slipped her other arm over her chest and around her ribs.

This was awkward at best.

Doc touched the right shoulder, pressing with seasoned fingers. The widow lurched, but her mother held firm. She kicked against Haskell, hard enough to break her own ankles, but she did not cry out.

He'd seen men fare far worse.

"It's not broken." Sweat beaded on the doctor's forehead. "Dislocated. Hold her, now. I'm going to pop it back in place."

Haskell squeezed. Mrs. Hutton leaned into her daughter. Doc Mason yanked.

The widow's eyes flew open as if she'd been shot, then she fell slack and her head lolled to the side, her mouth open. Out cold.

Haskell let go and shoved his shaking hands in his pockets. What was wrong with him?

Chapter 4

Martha sat at her dressing table, eyes closed, basking in Joseph's attention. He stood behind her, pulling the hand-painted brush through her hair with long, smooth strokes. Smiling, she lifted her eyes to meet his in the glass.

She gasped at the dark visage there, the ice-blue gaze that bore into her with an unsettling possessiveness. She squeezed her eyes shut and opened them again to see the parlor ceiling above her. Her parents' parlor. A sling secured her right arm to her chest and her feet flounced awkwardly over the short settee's armrest. She struggled to sit upright and a movement behind her warned of an approaching presence.

"Allow me."

A deeply tanned hand took hold of her left arm and steadied her as she pulled herself up and swung her feet to the floor. The effort spun her head like a top and she raised her left hand to her temple.

"Are you all right?"

Again, that voice. She leaned against the settee's back, gripping an armrest.

"I'll get you some water."

"I don't want any water." Her abruptness scratched her own ears and she glanced at the tall stranger standing in her parents' home, so committed to her well-being.

Training at a pastor's hand forced a quieter response. "But thank you."

The man's face bore the lines of one who squinted long and tirelessly into the sun. A deep indentation ringed his head, evidence of a hat normally worn over black collar-length hair. His shadowed jaw could have smoothed her nails if she dared raise them to it. She curled the fingers of her left hand and slid them beneath her skirt.

Determined to know, she softened her tone. "Who are you and why are you here?"

He pulled a footrest closer. Martha fully expected it to collapse beneath his weight, but it held him, though his knees pitched high, as if he were perched on a milk stool. In spite of his seating, he relaxed and the tension in his jaw loosened. "Haskell Jacobs, ma'am. I carried—brought you in from the street where you fell."

That explained the sling.

"Why are you here?"

He swallowed. "I brought you in—"

"I know that."

A blue gaze slashed across her.

She would not be intimidated. Not in her parents' home. "Why are you *here,* in Cañon City, Mr. Jacobs?"

The light dimmed as a shade drew down, shutting her out from what lay in those icy depths. "Business."

The next logical question jumped to her lips, but she bit it back.

She raised her chin. "I see."

Footsteps approached from the kitchen and her mother appeared with a tray. "A cup of tea is just what you need, Marti. I'm glad to see you've awakened."

Evidently Mama thought Mr. Jacobs needed one too, for three cups perched atop the tray as well as the silver sugar bowl and three spoons. She stopped at Martha's knee and held the tray, searching for signs of fever, illness, nerves, rash, pox—all the things a mother feared would overtake her offspring, regardless of their age.

"Thank you, Mama."

A weak smile. Her mother turned to Mr. Jacobs, whose hand dwarfed the teacup. Surprisingly skillful with the china, he declined the sugar and held the cup and saucer unwaveringly.

Those hands would swallow her hairbrush.

Betrayed by the uninvited image, Martha smarted at the heat in her face and bent her head to hide her humiliation.

Her mother took the chair to Martha's left, facing Mr. Jacobs. Silence encased them in a delicate web that Martha cared not to break herself. She sipped the hot tea. Chamomile, her favorite.

The sun slanted through lace curtains at the west window and cut ornate designs on the carpet. Her father would be home soon for supper. Shouldn't Mr. Jacobs be leaving?

Head down, she peeked at his boots, dusty and black like the rest of his attire, other than a gray shirt beneath his shadowed chin. A coat brush would do the man a world of good. Had he no wife to care for his clothes?

O Lord, help me. I am surely losing my mind.

Her head ached with the search for clear thought and one bobbed to the surface.

"The apron." She looked to Mr. Jacobs. "Did you see an apron?"

He stared as if she were a halfwit.

She stared back.

"Were you wearing an apron from the store?" Her mother's cup landed hard on the saucer.

Martha flinched. "No. I had rolled it up. It was in my hands, I think."

Mr. Jacobs retrieved his hat from beneath a chair and stood. "Thank you, Mrs. Hutton." He set his cup and saucer on the tray that waited on a side table and turned to Martha. "I'm glad to see you are feeling better. Next time, look both ways before you step into the street."

Fire rushed into her temples. How dare he speak down to her. She was not a child. *He* ran into *her*. She opened her mouth to set him straight when her mother rose. "Thank you, Mr. Jacobs, for bringing Marti home safely. I do appreciate your concern." She followed him to the door and clasped both hands at her waist.

He held out a silver piece.

"No, but thank you. We can cover the doctor's expenses. Really, it is not necessary."

He laid the coin next to the lamp by the front window, jerked his hat on and nodded to them both.

"Ma'am. Miss." Then he left.

Her mother ignored the silver, returned to Martha and sat next to her, reaching for her left hand. "I'm sure he meant well."

"I am sure he meant nothing of the sort."

The set of her mother's mouth forewarned a lecture. Martha withdrew her hand. She was not a child. Did both Mr. Jacobs and her mother see her as such?

"Marti—"

"Why do you insist on calling me that? I am not a schoolgirl. I am a grown woman, an *educated* woman."

That had not come out as she intended.

Her mother's face paled and her jawline tightened. She looked directly into Martha's eyes.

"Educated enough not to step in front of a man on horseback?"

Martha's anger evaporated.

"What if he had run you over? What if he had trampled you and left you in the street?"

The suggestion certainly described Martha's emotions at the moment. Tears clogged her throat and stung her eyes. She fingered the neck of her bodice.

Her mother's tone softened. "What were you thinking?"

At such gentleness, the barricade broke, and words gushed

out on a wrenching sob. "I was thinking of children—the children I will never have."

Martha leaned into her mother's embrace, much more a schoolgirl than a woman. "Oh, Mama, I don't know what I'm going to do. I thought I could go on without Joseph, but I can't. I've tried and everywhere I turn I think of him, of what might have been."

She pulled a hankie from her sleeve and held it to her eyes. "I'm sorry."

"You've been sorry quite long enough for something you've no need to apologize for. Is this what Joseph would want you to do—grieve your life away? Or would he want you to remember him for the good days you shared? Be the vibrant young woman he fell in love with?"

"At twenty-four I am no longer young or vibrant."

Her mother's brow knotted and she clutched her skirt in both fists as if fighting for Martha's life. "Start over, Marti—Martha."

The correction squeezed her heart anew. "But how could I ever love anyone other than Joseph?"

Again her mother reached out. "You make the fresh start and let the Lord take care of your heart, dear. Get involved at the mercantile or someplace else. Perhaps the Women's Reading Club. Maybe you could lead a children's group at church, or look into teaching at the school this winter. Or help your brother and Livvy up at the ranch. The twins are a handful for Livvy, you know."

Children. Always someone else's children. Or the mercantile.

Martha spread the damp hankie on her lap. "I don't want to be a storekeeper, but I know Grandma could use my help."

"And you could use hers. She knows what it means to lose your life's companion." Her voice thickened.

"I'm sorry, Mama. You must miss Grandpa terribly."

"I do. But I concentrate on what he gave me, not on what I lost when he passed on. My prayer is that you will do the same. Joseph is with the Lord whom you both love. Trust that God will lead you as you face the rest of your life."

Martha wrapped her arm about her mother's shoulders and kissed her graying temple. "I love you, Mama."

"I love you, too, dear. But not nearly as much as our Lord does."

Haskell strode down the short lane to Main Street, paused for a mule-drawn wagon and crossed to the other side. He snatched up a crumpled roll of white fabric and swiped at brown hoof marks imprinted on the sturdy cloth. It would take more than the brush of his hand to make it right.

His gut twisted like the cloth. Making things right involved more than the widow's apron. He wanted to make things right with her.

He was a fool.

Folding the roll in half, he turned up the street toward the laundry. If they couldn't get it clean and like new, he'd have another one made to replace it.

Decision made. The knot in his belly eased.

Life had been predictable and simple when he came to Cañon City. He had a man to find, a duty to do and a plan to carry it out.

And then that woman stepped off the train.

In the time it took to cock his pistol or cuff a wrist, his life had jumped the track.

He stomped into the laundry and slapped the apron on the counter. A sweaty little man rolled it out to its full length and gave Haskell the once-over.

"Can you make it look brand-new?"

The man's eyebrows dipped and he turned the cloth around. "Can do. Five cents."

"Today?"

"Tomorrow."

Haskell slammed a coin on the counter and turned to leave.

"Name!"

"Tillman."

His stomach pushed him toward the café.

Few patrons remained this late in the afternoon and he took the table against the back wall, the chair facing the door.

A thick man with thicker hair brought coffee and a heavy mug, and poured without asking. Haskell nodded his thanks.

"Beef stew's all we got left. And biscuits."

Haskell's mouth watered at the memory of the widow's biscuits and molasses. "That'll be fine."

The coffee was charred, but it jolted him back to reality.

He was old. Too old and too hard for a woman like the widow. At thirty-three he'd taken part in more than his share of brawls and killings, and he wouldn't know the first thing about settling down.

But that was what he'd been planning for the last few years. The exact reason he'd convinced the captain to let him take this job. He intended to scope out more than horse thieves and train jumpers. He wanted to drop his reins on a piece of cow country with a steady flowing creek and sweet grass. Grow a few fruit trees, raise a family. Stay in one place.

But men like him didn't get to live that kind of life.

The waiter returned with a steaming bowl and set it before him. "There's a little more where that come from if you're still hungry." He held out his hand. "Four bits. Coffee's on the house."

Haskell dropped a half dollar in the open palm. The man looked at the coin, glared at Haskell and left.

If the stew was palatable, he'd leave a short bit on the table.

The tack was cold and hard, but the well-seasoned beef and vegetables made up for it. He broke the bread into chunks and stirred them into the stew. Martha Hutton Stanton must be the only one around who could make a decent biscuit.

He jabbed at a chunk of meat and splashed gravy on the tablecloth. That woman wouldn't let him be. She drew him off course at every turn. He needed to find his man and leave town.

A half hour later he headed Cache toward the Arkansas and turned upstream. Cottonwoods grew thick and green along the banks and Canada geese poked through pastures that sloped down to the water's edge. Few fences blocked his path, but where they did, Cache easily took the lazy current at a slow walk. The water ran smooth and low this close to town, unlike the rapids farther up the canyon.

Again he reined Cache onto the bank. A canvas tent snugged against the trees and a dying fire sent wavering heat circling 'round a spider and tripod. A blackened coffeepot sat on the stones.

He called out.

An old man bent beneath the tent flap. From the looks of his hat and beard, a miner gone bust. He squinted at Haskell, stepped out and stood as straight as his old bones allowed.

"What kin I do fer ya?"

"You alone here?"

A bony hand slipped into the pocket of his dungarees. "Who wants to know?"

Haskell pulled his coat back, revealed the star on his vest. "I'm not looking for trouble. Just hunting a horse thief."

A grin cracked above the unshorn beard. "'Tain't me."

The other hand swept around the campsite. "As you kin see, I ain't got no horseflesh here." He bounced out a crackly laugh. "I hardly got any flesh o' my own."

The man hobbled to the fire, poked a stick under the coffeepot lid and peeked in. "I can give ya coffee and that's about it."

Haskell looked upstream. He should move on. Cache tossed his head in unspoken agreement. "I'll take you up on that offer." He stepped down and dropped the reins.

The grin widened and with a lighter step, the old-timer disappeared into the tent and returned with a tin cup. "Don't get many callers down here like in the old days." He pulled a rag from his pocket and lifted the pot.

Haskell straddled a log and took the offered cup. "Thank you."

The man retrieved another tin from behind the fire circle and poured himself a drink.

"Here's to good huntin', son." He raised the cup in a mock toast.

Haskell tested the brew with a cautious swallow. Second time today he'd been referred to as young. He snorted.

"Not to your likin'?" The old man's eyes narrowed.

"No, sir. It's fine. Just fine. I was thinking about something else."

A cackling laugh. "Outlaws or women?"

Haskell shot a glance at the man. He didn't need a prophet in the mix, but with different clothes, the old-timer fit the bill.

"Both are trouble, but one's more fun 'n the other."

Haskell took a swig of warm coffee. "I can't argue with you there."

The man wiped his coat sleeve across his bushy mustache. "Seen a fella walkin' the river last night leadin' a string o' mighty fine ponies. Didn't know I was watchin' him."

Haskell lowered his cup, focused on the old-timer's story.

"I figured he didn't own any of 'em. Otherwise, why sneak 'em by here after dark and not ride 'em through town in the daylight?"

"Was he headed upstream?"

"He was. Had a full moon last night and after he passed, I follered him. He walked near the length o' town before cuttin' off into the trees. I figured we was at the other end of Main Street by that time."

Haskell swirled the dregs. "Why'd you follow him?"

"Why not?" A toothy grin pushed through the whiskers. "Like I said, don't get many visitors out here nowadays and I figured he was up to no good. Wanted to make sure he didn't come back and cut my juggler."

Haskell tongued coffee grounds out of his cheek and set the cup on a rock. He pulled a silver dollar out of a vest pocket and laid it one rock over. "Thank you for the Arbuckle's."

The miner's eyes narrowed and he angled his head away, watching his guest out the side of his face. "What's that fer?"

"The coffee." Haskell stepped easy to his horse, aware of the old-timer's hand still in his pocket. He gathered the reins, swung into the saddle and touched his hat brim. "And the information."

The man reached for the coin and turned it over a couple of times before tucking it away.

Haskell rode upstream a half mile. At a clearing in the trees he turned toward Main Street and followed an overgrown trail that led to the barn behind Doc Mason's place.

Chapter 5

Martha's shoulder ached as she rolled to her left side and swung her feet over the edge of the bed. A restless night had left her weary and irritable. If Mr. Haskell Jacobs crossed her path today, she planned to tell him exactly what she thought of his horsemanship and his unseemly manners in the parlor yesterday.

And then she would stop thinking of him altogether.

Last night her mother had filled the copper tub with hot water and let her soak in luxury until the water cooled. It eased the pain and soothed her simmering temper, and she'd give almost anything to repeat the process this morning. But that was unlikely. One did not bathe in broad daylight in the kitchen.

At the washstand in her room she squeezed out a cloth with one hand and scrubbed her face and neck and shoulders—as much as possible. She needed her mother's help with her hair, her dress and her shoes. Grateful that she hadn't fallen on her left shoulder, she dipped a small brush in tooth powder and cleaned her teeth, then unfastened her braid and pulled it free. It hung over her shoulder and past her waist, and she pulled the brush through it, scraping the bristles against her body.

Joseph was gentler.

Would she ever complete the morning ritual without thinking of him?

You make the fresh start and let the Lord take care of your heart.

The words pushed against her memories, making room for themselves among other unpleasant reminders.

She'd thought the Lord *was* taking care of her heart. Yet all along He had known it would break when the bullet crashed into Joseph's skull.

Her chest tightened, and in the mirror she stared at the fossilized bones edging her bookcase across the room. If God were to open her rib cage and lift out what remained of her heart, He'd find it as cold and hardened as her stony collection. Lifeless.

A tap on her door. "Mar—*tha?*"

"Come in, Mama, I'm up."

Her mother walked straight to the window, pushed the curtains aside and opened the window as far as it would go. "It's stuffy up here. And dark."

Like me.

"May I help with your hair?"

Her mother waited, hands pressed flat against her apron as if holding herself back with an obvious effort. Would Martha act any differently if she were watching her own daughter flounder?

She'd never know. But that didn't mean she had to be unappreciative and difficult. "Would you, please?"

The relieved light on her mother's face nearly outshone the early sun. "How do you want it? Up or down?"

"Down. In a braid."

Martha closed her eyes against the pain. Each tug of her mother's nimble fingers pulled a stinging thread through her heart. As determined as she was to be independent, here she sat having her hair braided by the one who had done so before she could do it herself.

A cruel twist to come home bereft of husband and end up nearly helpless. She sighed heavily.

"Impatient?" Her mother smiled into the mirror. "I'm almost finished."

"No, that's not it at all. I'm frustrated. I feel absolutely helpless."

"I can imagine. You've always been so active." She tied a blue ribbon at the braid's end and then helped Martha into her dress and fastened it. "Let's turn this into an opportunity to get you a new dress."

"My trunk holds several skirts and blouses. I've just not shaken them out yet."

"And I'm sure they are lovely." Her mother walked to the door and paused as if waiting for Martha to follow. "But you are just as much a woman as I, and I know how it makes me feel when I get something new to wear."

The sparkle in her mother's eye won her over, and Martha stooped to pick up her shoes. "Only if you'll help me with these in the kitchen."

"Of course."

Martha handed over the shoes. At the stairs she gripped the handrail and headed down.

"Good morning, beautiful." From the kitchen table, her father smiled over the top of the *Cañon City Times*.

"Thank you, Papa." She kissed his cheek and pulled out a chair.

"I do believe your father was addressing his lovely wife." Her mother planted a smug smooch on his lips and tossed Martha a wink. "Hold up your foot."

She slipped one shoe over Martha's dark stocking and buttoned it, and then repeated the process, ending with a gentle pat against her ankle. "I have tea, Martha, if you prefer."

Sensing her father's curiosity over her given name, Martha avoided his eyes as she adjusted her sling to a more comfortable angle. "I'll take coffee this morning. I think I'm going to need it."

Her mother set three cups and saucers on the table, each bearing a delicate pink rose pattern rimming the edges.

"These are new—they're beautiful." She didn't miss the shy smile before her father hid once more behind the newspaper.

"Your father gave them to me for our wedding anniversary this year."

Martha reached for the sugar bowl. "How thoughtful of you, Papa."

The paper rattled. "I know."

Her laugh erupted on its own, startling her with its spontaneity. Laughter and humor had nearly rusted away from neglect. A thin fissure ran up the hard spot in her chest.

Hot cakes, eggs and bacon were more than she wanted, but she nibbled the bacon and managed a few bites of syrupy cake. "Will you be making apple butter this fall, Mama?"

"Oh, yes. Our trees are quite full. But the Blanchards—you remember them—invited us out to pick as much as we could haul home. They insist this year's crop is the best they've had in twenty."

Her father gathered his flatware, napkin and plate and took them to the sink. "I have an appointment this morning at the church, so I need to be off. What do you ladies have planned for today?"

He came up behind his wife and wrapped his arms around her, kissing the top of her head.

Martha lowered her eyes. The affection her parents had consistently shown one another over the years was something she had longed for in her own marriage. Joseph had loved her, had been loving in his own way during their brief marriage. But he'd not met her expectations as far as affection was concerned. Now that he was gone, guilt chewed on her raw edges. Was she simply greedy and ungrateful by nature?

"We are going to visit the dressmaker." Her mother leaned her head back against his chest and linked his arm with her fingers. "Who are you meeting so early?"

"Haskell Jacobs. Said he had something confidential he wanted to discuss with me about one of our citizens."

Martha stilled like an unwound watch, waiting for her breath to catch up and flow freely. Her father noticed.

"Don't be alarmed, Marti. It's just a meeting. But I do think there is more to Mr. Jacobs than meets the eye."

Her mother sobered instantly and stood to face him. "Why do you say that? Do you think he's an outlaw?"

Her father chuckled in the way men did when thinking they knew better than a woman. Guilt gnawed at Martha for categorizing her own father as such.

He looped his wife's waist with his hands and kissed her forehead. "I think he's a good man and I will give him the benefit of the doubt until he proves otherwise."

Martha snorted.

"I won't turn my back on him, Marti, but I'm not often wrong about reading people. They are a lot like horses, you know."

Immediately a long-eared equine relative came to mind, but she knew better than to voice her uncomplimentary vision of Haskell Jacobs. Her father gave her a light peck and headed through the house for the front door.

Doc Mason had been as forthcoming yesterday as Haskell expected: not at all. His assistant was worse. He'd never seen such a sour look on a woman's face, as if his questions insulted her own kin.

Which led to a different perspective. He passed up the sheriff and other ministers in town, and caught Reverend

Hutton exiting the mercantile. His gut told him Caleb Hutton was the man to see.

The preacher agreed to meet at the white clapboard church house this morning at eight sharp. Haskell flipped open his watch. Five minutes till.

He planted an elbow on the church hitching rail and watched the horses corralled across the street. Cache held his own in the livery pecking order and a lightning-quick kick sent a surly mare on her way. Haskell grunted.

At a metallic click he turned. The front door opened and Hutton stopped on the threshold. "Right on time. Come in."

Haskell mounted the steps and pulled off his hat. "Thank you for meeting me this morning, Pastor."

"Caleb." The parson extended his hand in greeting. "I'm more comfortable on a first-name basis." A genuine smile warmed his features. No snake oil dripped from the corners of his mouth.

Haskell felt oddly at ease, considering how long it had been since he'd been in a church.

Sunlight filtered through the eastside windows, buttering the pews with a yellow glow. Hutton walked to the front of the room and sat in the first pew, turning slightly to the side. Haskell joined him—again, hat in hand. It was getting to be a bad habit.

"I'd like to begin by telling you I know what happened yesterday with my daughter."

Haskell slid his lawman's mask across his eyes and gave no response one way or the other. He had yet to categorize the parson, and a father's reaction to his daughter's injury was not to be underestimated.

"Thank you for bringing Marti home and fetching the doctor."

At that, Haskell's jaw eased a notch and he let his gaze slide to his hat. "I'm sorry about the accident. I should have—"

"That is exactly what it was, I believe. An accident." The preacher's dark eyes drank in every inch of Haskell's face but didn't give away his own thoughts. The man had the makings of a ranger. He crossed a boot on his leg and stretched one arm along the pew back. "You wanted to ask me something."

Haskell dangled his hat on his fingers. "How is she doing today?" The question surprised him as much as it did the preacher.

The preacher smiled politely. "She's her old sharp self. A little stiff, that's all. I expect she'll be slowing more at the street corners now." The smile waned. "But that can't be what you had on your mind yesterday afternoon."

No, it wasn't. He just wished it were. He pulled his coat back to reveal the star. Hutton caught the movement without surprise. He'd probably heard and seen just about everything in his line of work.

"I'm with the Colorado Rangers out of Denver, and I'm looking for a horse thief who's said to hole up in these parts."

"There are a lot of places for a man to hide around here. Plenty of abandoned mines and narrow canyons in this country."

"Yes, sir. But you might know him."

The preacher's right eye twitched.

"Without knowing he's a thief."

Hutton uncrossed his leg. "How do you figure? Think he's one of my congregants?"

"I think he's connected to Doc Mason."

Both eyes twitched and the preacher rubbed the back of his neck.

"I rode along the river yesterday afternoon and came upon an old man camped back in the cottonwoods. He told me a fella traipsed through the night before with a string of four good horses. Said he followed him and the man turned toward town at the other end of Main Street."

Hutton nodded. "That would be Goldpan Parker you met. Went bust years ago, but seems content to live down there on the river." He looked hard at Haskell. "But if there were strange horses in town I'd know it. And I haven't seen any."

"No, you haven't seen them. They're stabled in Doc Mason's barn. Four nice head, haltered and filling themselves on mountain hay."

Hutton held his gaze.

"I followed Parker's lead, ended up at Mason's barn and looked inside." The partial truth jabbed Haskell in the preacher's presence. "I went inside. That's when I saw the fresh brand on their shoulders, recently burned with a running iron."

"You think Mason's a horse thief?" Hutton squinted.

"No, I don't. But I think he's housing one. When I rode down there yesterday to bring him back for Marti—I mean your daughter—Doc and his nurse were working on a fella in the surgery. I didn't see him, but I could hear him. He was hurting. When the nurse came out she was curt and hostile. Had a bloody towel in her hands. She and the Doc had been talking about laudanum and I heard them shuffling someone to another room before she came out to see me.

Hutton frowned and rubbed his neck again. "Have you talked to the doctor?"

"Yesterday before I found you. He wouldn't tell me anything about his patients. Said he couldn't talk about them, even if they were outlaws or horse thieves. Especially to people who weren't kin."

"Does he know you're a ranger?"

"Yes."

Hutton blew out a breath. "I'm bound by a similar standard. I can't talk about other people's problems and troubles. But I can tell you this much—the nurse is Delores Overton. Several years ago her son Tad got himself shot during the Railroad War here between the Denver & Rio Grande and the Santa Fe. A lot of good men got caught up in that, but there was always something about her boy Tad that didn't set right with me."

"Can you put your finger on it now?"

A shadow crossed Hutton's face and he turned his gaze toward the windows.

Haskell clenched his jaw and waited. He needed information.

"We sent Marti away to school about that time. She was sweet on him."

But not that kind of information.

Chapter 6

Martha cleared the table, scrubbed the counter and returned each piece of china to the dining room hutch—work that required only one hand. She placed the delicate dishes just so, arranging them as her mother had, obviously proud of such finery.

"Let's walk to the dressmaker's, Mama. It's been so long since I've done anything physical—other than stepping in front of a horse."

Her mother hung her apron on a hook and tucked a smile between her lips. "We shall stay to the boardwalks this morning. How does that sound?"

"Wonderful. And let's stop in at Mr. Winton's curio shop. I want to ask if he is still taking people up to the dig." She noted her mother's frown. "Is his shop still open?"

"Oh, yes. And he is still exhibiting remarkable fossils from the Garden Park before they are boxed and shipped out on the train to the university. But going to the dig in your condition could be dangerous, and not just because of the footing. Vandals are smashing some of the bones, and poor Mr. Finch—the farmer who's leading the dig—is beside himself. Plus he lost another son since you've been gone."

Martha stiffened at the news. Not uncommon to lose a child, but grieving over one's beloved children must be worse than grieving over children never born.

"Mr. Finch reopened the second quarry across from the

first one and Yale sent a paleontologist to help him with his work. But from what I hear, the site may be exhausted."

Old dreams stirred in Martha's heart as she and her mother left through the front door. She had to make it out to the dig at least once before it was shut down, sore shoulder or not.

Her mother swept her with a worried look. "Are you sure you're up to walking today? We can just as easily take the buggy."

"Nonsense. I am fine and I need the exercise." At the edge of Main Street, she glanced toward the open church door. Haskell Jacobs sat inside with her father talking about—what?

She huffed a short laugh. It did not matter. She twisted her reticule drawstring around the fingers of her left hand and stepped up her pace. "My arm is not broken. Doc Mason said as much. Maybe this sling is too confining and I should be working out the stiffness." She tugged at the knot behind her neck.

"Leave that be." Her mother's hand swatted hers away. "You don't want to make matters worse. Give it a week and we'll have the doctor check it again."

A week. In a week she'd lose what little of her mind remained if she did not find some outlet for her restlessness.

They turned left and kept to the south side of the street. Smart storefronts replaced what Martha remembered, and several new establishments boasted brightly painted signs. In the next block they turned in at the dressmaker's, which looked like a shop straight from St. Louis.

Evidence of scented soap and sachet hit Martha square in the face as they entered, but it did not overwhelm her any more than did the countless hats, parasols, gloves, reticules and petticoats that covered every inch of counter, wall and shelf space. Women clustered in every nook and cranny, chattering over the latest fashions and patterns.

Her mother laughed. "It is surprising, isn't it? I reacted just the same the first time I visited with your grandmother."

Martha didn't know what to consider first—material for a dress or a new hat. With feathers, ribbons or lace? Nothing in the store said *schoolmarm,* that was for sure. They headed for the back where fabric lay stacked on the counter.

Her mother picked up a length of lightweight wool and held it next to Martha's face. "This would be lovely with your hair."

The exact color of Haskell Jacobs's eyes.

And what if it was? He was not the only blue-eyed man in the world. Just the only one to have captured her attention.

Martha tugged at a dull gray. "What about this?"

Her mother dropped her hands to her side and pegged Martha with a warning glare.

"Must I spell it out for you? I'm trying to cheer you. Look at this place." She twirled around like a girl in a candy store. "Have you ever seen anything like this?"

Martha picked up the blue fabric and held it to her chin. "Five lengths?"

While they waited for Martha's turn to be measured and sized, they fondled delicate thread for tatting, several soft yarns and the most beautiful hair combs Martha had ever seen. Her mother pushed thoughtfully at the combs she had worn since time immemorial and Martha made a mental note for Christmas.

By the time the seamstress finished, Martha's stomach was growling like a cur. "I'm starving, Mama. Let's save the curio shop for another day and go home for dinner."

Outside, her mother linked arms with her and turned toward the heart of town. "Let's not." She marched up the boardwalk and Martha was obliged to follow. "I've heard about the wonderful food at the café. I think we should give it a try. What do you say?"

Apparently, it mattered not what Martha might say, for they were already at the corner, stepping into the street. She quickly looked to her left and flexed her right arm, which shot a pointed reminder to her shoulder.

"But what about Papa?"

Her mother chuckled. "Did I ever tell you how he lived before we were married?"

"Yes, you've told me." That rhetorical question had been discussed countless times during Martha's younger years. "I could recite it by heart."

"Well, then, no need to ask. I dare say your father will fend for himself. It's not every day I get to step out on the town with my daughter."

A departing couple exited the café as Martha and her mother approached, and a most delicious aroma followed them out the door. Martha's empty stomach noticed and she pushed against her waist to stop the rumbling.

A waiter seated them at a window table in clear view of the busy street and boardwalk. Fewer freight wagons rumbled by than she remembered, no doubt replaced by the train that cut through the mountain to Leadville and points beyond.

"We shall have whatever it is that smells so delightful," her mother said.

Martha turned her attention to the waiter who poured coffee into two mugs.

"It's pork chops, ma'am, with gravy and beans and potatoes."

"Wonderful." She looked at Martha for confirmation.

At the moment, Martha could eat almost anything. "Perfect," she said. "May I have extra gravy, please?"

The mustached waiter smiled and bowed briefly before turning on his heel for the kitchen. Amused by the man's formal attitude, Martha relaxed and reached for her coffee. She lifted it to her lips and looked up. With a sharp intake she jerked and coffee splashed onto the checkered cloth.

Her mother leaned toward her, worry darkening her eyes. "What is it? Are you all right?"

Martha set down the mug and dabbed at the stain with her napkin. "I'm fine." She shot a glance over her mother's shoulder, relieved that Haskell Jacobs was too busy dismembering his pork chops to notice her. At least she hoped so.

She scooted her chair to the left and met her mother's concerned gaze, which now blocked her view of the arrogant Mr. Jacobs. "I just recognized someone I did not expect to see, that's all."

Her mother turned.

"Mama!"

She stopped at Martha's frantic whisper and cocked a thin brow. "And why not?"

"It's Mr. Jacobs. I don't want him to see me." She'd said too much.

Her mother leaned back in her chair and tilted her head. "Is your father with him?"

"No."

Martha squirmed again, feeling like a schoolgirl beneath her mother's scrutiny. The woman expected some sort of confession, admission of, of…what? Martha would gladly bare her soul if only she understood the situation herself.

Haskell saw them enter the café. He saw *everyone* who entered the café. It was his job to be aware, take note. But his bucking pulse at Marti Hutton's arrival was not.

He busied himself with the meat, forked a bite in the gravy and kept his head low as he chewed. Haskell Jacobs backed down to no man. So why did he react to the presence of the young widow wearing a sling?

Maybe it was the sling. He'd been thinking of her and not paying attention when she stepped in front of Cache yesterday morning. Distraction could get him killed. It nearly got her killed.

He cut off another bite and stole a look. She caught his eyes and flinched. Spilled her coffee. The mere sight of him distressed her.

He looked again. She had moved to her left, positioned her mother between them.

The meat turned to wood in his mouth and he laid down his fork. He was not a man to run from trouble, and this situation with Marti Hutton or Martha Stanton or whatever her name was, was trouble. It was taking its toll on him, costing him precious time and dulling his observational skills.

Decision made. He'd take the apron to her this afternoon and confront her head-on.

About what, he had no idea.

He caught the waiter's eye, paid for his meal and tugged his hat down as he left. Outside on the boardwalk he blew out a breath, feeling he'd escaped a fate worse than being shot. A strange sensation.

He loosened Cache's reins from the hitching rail, swung up and rode toward the west end. He needed to think about something other than the widow and her one-time affection for a possible horse thief.

Tad Overton. The pastor said his son, Whit, knew the man. Whit ran cattle about ten miles out of town and a visit appealed to Haskell. Might give him a chance to see the country, maybe locate a few acres that needed a new owner.

But did he want to settle in Cañon City near a woman who drove every reasonable thought from his head and made him weak in the knees?

He slowed Cache to a walk at Doc Mason's. A buggy waited in front and the surgery door was open. Busy man.

The prison walls rose ahead, and a ways beyond them, across the river, the Hot Springs Hotel. Fifty cents bought a bath in the thermal waters. The steamy image appealed to him—a good hot soaking after dark, followed by a slow walk behind Mason's barn on the way back to the St. Cloud.

He turned north up First Street and rode in the shadow of the penitentiary walls. Seemed like a waste of time to drag a horse thief back to Denver when Haskell could just as easily chuck him over the high stone battlement. He grunted at the idea. Quite a sight for the town's residents.

But due process was due process. Even a thief deserved a trial.

Grand homes faced the shady streets running north of and parallel to Main, and Haskell passed fanciful structures of rose quartz and granite. Two- and three-story houses boasted yellow or green gingerbread, reminiscent of Denver's grandeur. Much gaudier than the Huttons' parsonage with its simple white clapboard and broad porch.

His house would have a porch. And a swing for summer evenings when the sun washed coppery gold over the Rockies. And a wife with hair the same color.

He kicked Cache into a lope, disgusted with his slack discipline. The sooner he got the chore over with, the better. He yanked the horse around the corner nearest the laundry, dismounted and stomped inside.

Voices chattered from behind a wide curtain, but no one manned the darkened storefront. His hand slapped the counter and the voices stilled. The curtain moved, and dark eyes peeked through a slit, followed by the fellow who had told him the apron would be ready today.

The little man pulled a bundle from below the counter and handed it to Haskell.

"Thank you." He strode to the door, then stopped and turned. "Was it ruined?"

"Just dirty." The washer man grinned. "Now clean."

Haskell nodded and shut the door, then pulled the reins from the post and swung up.

By late afternoon, traffic had thinned and the board-walk emptied. He tied Cache at the livery, tucked the parcel under his arm and walked to the parsonage. The widow sat on the porch swing and stopped its motion when she saw him.

He, too, stopped, expecting her to flee indoors to her mother. Instead, she pushed against the porch floor and resumed the swing's movement. His heart resumed beating.

"Evening," he said as he took the steps and stood before her.

The widow looked at the bundle. "Good evening, Mr. Jacobs."

No wind whisper or prairie sigh tonight. Her tone raised a wall as cold and stony as the prison's. He held out the paper-wrapped package. "Here's your apron."

Surprise raised her brows. She stopped the swing again and reached out with her left hand. A question lit her face and rather than wait for her to ask, he answered.

"I had it laundered."

She looked at him with something near gratitude before tucking the expression safely inside. "I see that."

What had he expected?

He turned on his heel. He wasn't going to apologize.

"Please, won't you have a seat?"

Her offer stopped him and he looked over his shoulder. She held out a delicate white hand, indicating a chair at the end of the porch. For reasons beyond his comprehension, he followed her suggestion.

His boot steps echoed on the old wood, drawing him out into the open. Away from the shadows. He sat.

She laid the bundle on the swing and looked at him. Then she raised her eyes to his hat. He removed it and hung it on one knee. She almost smiled.

"Thank you for finding the apron and having it cleaned."

He could nearly hear the top stone layer crumbling from her wall. "My pleasure, ma'am."

"You may call me Martha."

Another layer toppled and he risked a question. "Is it Stanton or Hutton?" Hearing the query aloud convinced him it was none of his business.

She considered her lap, rolled her lips as if holding something back. He was a fool.

"That is a very good question, Mr. Jacobs." She lifted her gaze to the back of the church house a few yards beyond the front gate. "I began as Hutton, spent a short while as Stanton, and now I am Hutton again." She turned her focus to him, bold and unembarrassed, just as she had at the train station. Had it been only three days and not his entire life that she haunted his thoughts and clouded his mind?

Wicked and deadly men had dared look him in the eye and none had the effect of this injured woman. The linen sling mocked him.

"How is your shoulder?"

She tilted her head to the right and the guileless gesture shot an unwelcome dart of sympathy through him.

"Stiff, but that is to be expected. The sling is bothersome and it seems I can do nothing but sit and think."

"I am sorry."

Her gaze flicked sideways, but she quickly recovered. "Thank you, sir. I should not have plunged into the street without looking."

Now it was his turn to be surprised. The steel in his jaw melted like an icehouse afire.

"It's Haskell."

Chapter 7

Martha stilled before the blue scrutiny, cool and clear as a mountain lake. So much for her resolve to rebuke the mysterious Mr. Jacobs. He'd been headed off the porch and out of her life. Why had she stopped him?

"The name's Haskell," he repeated.

Quite aware of her tendency to stare, she forced her eyes down. "Haskell it is, then."

The screen door creaked and her father stepped outside. "I did not realize we had a caller, Marti." He crossed in front of her and offered his hand in greeting.

Haskell stood. "Sir."

"What brings you by, Mr. Jacobs?"

"Haskell, sir, if you don't mind."

The parson nodded and threw a quizzical glance at his daughter. "Have you invited our visitor for supper? I'm sure your mother has plenty, and I happen to know she has a peach pie set aside."

Martha's stomach clinched and all reasonable thought fled. Invite the man to supper? She cut him a look as he put his hat on and moved toward the porch steps. "By all means, Mr.—Haskell—please, stay to supper."

He looked at her father as if testing the water, then jerked a nod. "Thank you."

Her father offered his right arm to help her rise from the swing. "Let's not keep your mother waiting, Marti." His mouth quirked at one end, a sign she recognized all too well. A joke was at play and she was more than likely the brunt of it. She had half a mind to tell Haskell Jacobs to go eat with his horse. But when he stepped forward and held the screen door open, she swallowed the words.

Papa was right about the peach pie. Its flaky aroma threaded around her empty belly. She hadn't eaten much at dinner after noticing a certain man at the opposite end of the café. Now she had to face that man at her parents' table. *Lord, help me.*

"Annie, you remember Haskell Jacobs," her father said. "He's agreed to share our supper this evening."

Her mother turned a startled expression on the three of them but softened it with her usual grace. "How good of you, Mr. Jacobs. Caleb, please bring another chair from the dining room."

Martha moved to her place at the table but their guest anticipated her. He pulled the chair back, waited for her to seat herself, and then gently assisted her in scooting forward.

Her mind swirled like a river eddy. What kind of man meets privately with her father, pays good money to launder an old apron, holds her chair—and looks like the dark and handsome villain in a dime novel? Not that she ever read such things.

She pulled the napkin onto her lap and her mental ledger to the forefront. He'd even apologized for something she was at least partially responsible for. That final admission tugged her chin down in chagrin. Four marks for Haskell in the positive column and one in the negative for running her down with his horse. Two, maybe. His dark demeanor could be viewed as secretive. But *handsome* might slip into the number five slot on the other side.

Unfaithfulness jabbed a pointed finger as Joseph's fair image dimmed.

Her father returned. Haskell waited until Martha's mother was seated before taking his own chair.

Circumstances were against her. Or was it God? She pleaded silently that her parents break with their custom of holding hands in prayer and her plea was denied. Her mother sat across from Martha, to her father's right. This forced their guest to the end, placing Martha between the men.

Her father laid a hand on her right arm. She hesitated. At an arched warning from her mother, she lifted her left hand to Haskell who took it in his as if it were the most natural thing in the world.

Well, he had held her in his arms like a sack of flour. He might as well hold her hand.

Her neck warmed. If her pulse flashed through her fingers as it did her throat, he'd know and she would die of humiliation right there at the table.

"Amen."

With blood pounding in her ears, she hadn't heard her father's prayer and sat momentarily frozen. Haskell raised his brows in question and she jerked her hand from his. Laughter sparked in his eyes. Would it be completely inhospitable to stab him with her fork?

After the tasty remains of a beef stew, her mother dished up large servings of warm pie and passed around a pitcher of cream. With a childhood favorite before her, Martha almost forgot her current predicament—until she lifted her fork and realized that Haskell Jacobs was observing her.

She cut through a golden slice of peach.

"I'm going to take you up on your advice, sir, and visit your son, Whit."

"Good." Her father poured cream over his pie and set the small white pitcher in the center of the table. "I'm sure he can give you solid information."

Martha and her mother exchanged an unspoken question and waited for the men to reveal what lay behind their cryptic conversation.

They said nothing.

She had never been good at keeping her thoughts to herself, especially as far as her brother was concerned. "About?"

Haskell flashed a blue glance and set down his coffee. "I am looking for someone and your father believes Whit may be able to give me some insight into this person's behavior."

That was about as unspecific an explanation as she had ever heard. Her left hand paused against the table's edge, peach juice dripping from the fork tines onto her rose-edged plate. She looked to her father with expectation, years of practice ensuring that he sensed her curiosity.

He ignored her, continued eating his pie and addressed her mother.

"Weren't you thinking of driving out to visit Whit and Livvy and the boys, dear?" Innocence pooled around his eyes as thick as the cream around his peaches. She had never thought of her father as one to hedge. And she had learned long ago that leaving in a huff was most undignified, as was stomping one's foot beneath the table. It took everything in her to do neither.

Her mother shot Martha a peculiar look. "Yes, I was, but I'd not had opportunity to talk it over with Martha, see if she felt up to riding out to visit her nephews." She paused, teacup in hand, watching Martha over its edge.

Felt up to? Her mother had thrown down a gauntlet, and Martha was certain she had done it deliberately. She despised prissy women who feigned frailty as the weaker sex and her mother knew it. The woman had imbued her with the opinion, for goodness' sake.

She pulled herself straighter, adjusted the sling and

smoothed her lips into a sickeningly sweet smile. "I'd love to. We could go tomorrow."

"Perfect."

She stared at her enthusiastic father.

"Perhaps you wouldn't mind Haskell riding along with the both of you. You could show him the way, and he could serve as a sort of escort."

Martha's jaw must have banged against the table, but she could not help it. Never had either her mother or she ever been *escorted* to Whit and Livvy's. She stole a glance at Haskell who wore a mask as impenetrable as hammered steel.

By the meal's end, conversation had swayed from picking apples and the price of hay to the start of school and a basket social planned at the church, with Haskell invited, of course.

Martha rose to help her mother clear the table. Haskell stood as she did but did not retake his seat. Instead he lifted his hat from the back of his chair.

"Thank you, ma'am, Pastor, for sharing your supper." He nodded to Martha. "Miss Martha."

Her father led him to the front door. Martha stole to the parlor entry and waited on the kitchen side, out of view.

"I hope you find what you're looking for here in Cañon City." Her father paused. "I know I did."

Haskell mumbled something low that Martha could not decipher and then left.

She hurried back to the table and grabbed the empty pie tin before her father reappeared. Combing through her family history, she searched for what he had found in Cañon City. She came up with two items: his renewed calling and his wife.

The Hutton women's cooking could pull a man's heart out through his gullet and plop it in his plate. Haskell crossed the street to Cache, who stood dozing at the livery rail with a back leg cocked. He stripped the reins and swung up, hoping the hot springs bathhouse hadn't closed for the evening.

The prospect of accompanying the widow and her mother to Whit Hutton's ranch held all the promise and curse of a double eagle: a valuable commodity a man could lose his life over.

He rode out of town and followed the railroad tracks to the mouth of the gorge where a path veered toward a footbridge suspended across the river. He tethered Cache at a railing with two other horses and took to the plank bridge. Halfway across, he stopped and peered over the side at the dark water. The steady wash raised a voice unheard unless one stood close enough. Constant, steady. Changing in volume only as the seasons changed their colors, he surmised. Raging with spring floods, whispering beneath an icy mantle. Persistent, nonetheless. Always there.

Lights flickered through the hotel's windows and he continued toward them.

Not much was constant in his life, other than the hunt for those who broke the law. Again an unnamed longing surged through his soul, a swollen stream of discontent. But its churning did not soothe him. It merely emphasized his isolation.

The Royal Gorge Hot Springs Hotel offered a bath for fifty cents and he bought two. Rumors and pamphlets had been right. The thermal waters eased the tension in his neck and shoulders and back. If Cache were not waiting across the bridge, Haskell would rent a room and spend the night.

As it was, his relaxed legs barely carried him back across the footbridge.

Accustomed to the cool evenings of the Rocky Mountains in early fall, Haskell wakened enough to mount his horse and ride for town with a clear plan. At First Street he turned south and paralleled the river to the overgrown path he'd followed the day before.

He ground-tied Cache and then moved soundlessly through the trees toward Doc Mason's barn. A dim light glowed between the siding slats, and tense voices rose within.

"You won't be bringing any more horses to this barn. Do you hear me?" Doc Mason's high-pitched tones quivered with anger. Haskell picked his way through the leaves and fallen branches behind the barn and stopped near the back door, closed but leaking light at its edges. A lantern on the far wall backlit the doctor's face and that of a taller, slightly built man. A cloth bound the taller man's right thigh, and he held his hand fisted against it.

"They aren't here, are they?" The thin man gestured wildly toward the empty stalls and flinched at the effort.

"I don't care. I won't have stolen horses in my barn. And you should be in bed with that gunshot wound." Doc cursed and took the lantern from the wall. Shadows fell across their faces but in the lowered light Haskell saw the shine of blood oozing through the thin man's bandage.

"That ranger was asking about you yesterday. I should have let him haul you off. Would have, if it weren't for your ma."

Haskell ground his teeth. The doctor just incriminated himself in harboring a fugitive. And Haskell's hunch about the nurse had also been right. But he needed evidence, and without the horses, witnesses or a direct confession, he had nothing.

Pastor Hutton's hunch had panned out. Tad Overton was his man, and as far as Haskell could tell, the lanky man favoring his right leg was none other.

Doc left the barn and Overton followed.

A horse nickered out front—Doc's buggy nag, more

than likely. Haskell stole around the far end of the barn and up to the corral where the horse twitched an ear his way. Doc and Overton went up the back porch steps and inside, and the light dimmed as they made their way to the front of the house.

Those four stolen horses could be anywhere by now. Overton could have sold them to the Utes or the hack owners who carted people back and forth to the hot springs. A rancher could have run them in with his own band, turning a blind eye to the new shoulder burns.

He retraced his steps to Cache and led the horse downstream to a clearing where he mounted and continued to the livery.

Would Whit Hutton buy stolen horses?

Haskell doubted it. Something about that family felt strong and true, like a deep-running current that held them all together. But he'd find out for himself in less than twelve hours, for tomorrow morning he was accompanying the Hutton women to the ranch.

Crickets raised a chorus. A dog yelped and a gate hinge squeaked. Ahead of him a yellow orb inched above the horizon like an out-of-place sun. He pulled up to watch.

The full moon hefted itself against the night, appearing bigger at the horizon's edge than it would later as it mounted the sky. Haskell chuckled to himself at the phenomenon that had puzzled him as a child.

"It's all in your eye," his father had said. "It's no different when it starts than when it reaches its zenith."

His father had him hold a penny at arm's length, right next to the rising moon, and note its size. Together they'd spent the night on bedrolls by a campfire—Haskell and the man he admired most in the world, Tillman Jacobs, Jefferson Ranger.

Hours later, his father woke him. The moon dangled from the night like an empty saucer.

"Hold out your penny," his father had said.

Haskell would never forget the sense of discovery that washed over him when he lifted the copper coin and saw the moon was the same size as it had been when it first peeked through the pines.

"That's called perspective, son. Things are not always as they appear. Judge wisely—with evidence—and you will do well."

Those words still guided him. Haskell had spent most of his life pursuing that first taste of discovery. That thrill of uncovering the hidden or solving an enigma. It was the drive that pushed him to be a ranger, like his father, and it fueled his determination to find those who spurned the law and to see justice done.

Anticipation gripped his insides. Tomorrow would bring him closer to the horse thief he sought. And closer to the complex Martha Hutton Stanton, now Hutton again, as she had put it. A day in her company might wreak havoc with his powers of observation, for if he admitted the truth to himself, he was drawn to pursue her as surely as he pursued the snake that stole another man's horse and profited from it.

The copper-haired beauty pulled him like night pulled the moon across the sky.

He had to get Whit Hutton alone, away from the women, and talk to him in private. Hutton might have a tip on the horses, information connecting Overton to them or word of their whereabouts.

Without a sound lead, Haskell had no grounds to bring Tad Overton in.

And if he did make a viable connection, what would Martha think of him then—when he rode away with her former beau in handcuffs?

Chapter 8

Sitting in the parlor as her father read by lamplight and her mother darned socks was absolutely out of the question. What was Martha supposed to do? Stare out the windows into the night and fume?

Betrayed. Bested. Beaten. A vocabulary list formed in her mind, filling with words disloyal to the parents who had raised her and loved her. But they still tried to control her. She stood and walked to the door where she paused at the screen and breathed in the night air.

"I'm going to sit outside for a while." Without waiting for a reply, she escaped to the porch swing and fell into its restful arms. Haskell's tall presence seemed to linger on the porch where he had sat earlier in the day.

If she had not allowed herself to be baited into inviting him to supper, he would not be "escorting" them to Whit and Livvy's tomorrow. How could her father do such a thing? What had he and Haskell discussed that morning that so influenced his opinion of the man?

She huffed at the memory of Haskell's vague explanation. If one of her former students had given such a nonanswer to a direct question, she'd have kept the student after class to beat erasers.

She toed the swing and forced her thoughts to her nephews. She had seen the twins only in a cabinet card her brother had sent one Christmas, and then they were babes in their mother's arms. They were nearly seven years old now, a handful, her mother had said. But, as boys, they must be Whit's delight. Surely he had them riding and roping already.

A child-shaped emptiness throbbed in her soul.

Bitterness was taking hold there. She recognized it as clearly as she'd recognized the horseradish that grew behind the small parsonage she shared with Joseph. If even a mite of that ugly tuber remained in the soil, it sprouted. Oh, how she had worked to rid her garden of it.

A scripture ran through her mind, warning her to weed out the vicious root. Was bitterness defiling her, and her family as well, as the passage suggested?

"Oh, Lord, help me." These seemed the only words she prayed since Joseph's death. Did God hear? She'd been raised to believe so.

"Help me dig out the bitterness," she whispered into the darkness. "Help me accept barrenness as readily as Whit has accepted the blessing of children."

Bitter. Barren. Blessing. More words for the new list.

Her mother's soft laughter floated through the screen door and Martha stopped the swing to listen. Now she could add eavesdropping to her catalogue of sins.

"He is a good man, Annie. I am sure of it."

Who? Martha scooted to the end of the swing closest to the door.

"But he is so secretive," her mother said. "Did you notice how he avoided Martha's question at the table?"

Haskell. Martha held her breath.

"He has good reason."

"And that is?"

Not a word. Only the whisper of evening through the giant elm in the front yard.

Her mother huffed.

"Why are you calling her Martha now?" Her father's tone had changed, softened.

"Because it is her wish. She does not want us considering her a child, and the name we used in her youth makes her think we still see her that way."

"I will always see her as my child—my lively, fiery beauty."

Martha covered her mouth to squelch a sob.

Her father's voice lowered into rich tones meant only for his wife.

Again, her mother's soft laughter. "Oh, Caleb."

All too well Martha knew the intimate moments between a woman and her husband, and her mother's voice betrayed such tenderness. She rose from the swing and slipped through the door and onto the stairs. Once behind the safety of her closed door, she fell onto the bed and cried until she slept.

The morning sun slid beneath a cloud bank, as reluctant to rise as Martha was to leave her quilts. Her shoulder ached again from lying on it in the night, and she pushed herself up, rubbing at the soreness.

Her pitcher held warm water—her mother's doing. Martha had been no help since her arrival, thwarted first by sorrow and now by injury. And she still hadn't found anything to do. The schools had a full roster of teachers this late in the year, but she could check at the library. Someone there might be interested in her scientific studies or her sketching. She could teach basic drawing if nothing else.

Or mind the store.

Never.

As if stirring banked coals, the thought fanned her irritation over a predetermined future. She would find her own way. Even if she did need help to fasten her dress, button her shoes and comb her hair.

She tucked her brush into the sling and, clasping her shoes in one hand, descended the stairs in her stocking feet. Of all days to ride out to Whit's, it had to be cool and cloudy. Sunshine would have felt so good on her face. Yet the possibility remained that the clouds might burn off and not bank against the mountains into a late rainstorm.

There was hope.

The word fluttered soft against her spirit like a falling aspen leaf.

"Good morning." Her father took her shoes and offered his arm as he led her to the kitchen table. "Would you like me to nail these on for you?" His brow furrowed in his best mock frown.

Martha snatched them back. "No, thank you. I am not a horse." She kissed his cheek before taking her seat. "Mama, have you already fed the chickens and gathered eggs?"

"Yes, dear. How many do you want for breakfast?"

Martha huffed, drawing her mother's puzzled look.

"One, please. But you must let me make myself useful. I think I can manage tossing scraps to the hens and gathering eggs until my shoulder is ready for heavier tasks."

Her mother set a cup of tea before her with one hand and filled her father's coffee cup with the other.

"So you're off to Whit and Livvy's today." He lifted his cup.

How could a man be so totally guilty and innocent-looking at the same time?

"I do believe Mama and I could have made it out there without an escort." Martha watched closely to determine her father's mood.

His expression remained placid, unaffected. She gathered her nerve. "Why do we need Mr. Jacobs to accompany us when we safely made the trip dozens of times before I left for school?"

One brow flicked up and his eyes darkened further. "It is he who needs *your* accompaniment."

At the remark, her mother turned to face him, a question clearly about to crest her lips.

"But enough of that." He stood, took his cup to the sink and planted a kiss on his wife's neck.

Martha's heart pulled at the familiar gesture, something she had always wanted Joseph to do. But he simply had not had her father's spontaneity when it came to affection.

"Off with you," her mother fussed, pushing at the thick knot of hair at her neck, her cheeks tinted with a becoming rose. "If you are not going to stay and eat a good breakfast, then don't be distracting us in our preparations to leave."

"A distraction now, am I?" Martha's father aimed the question at her as he lifted his hat from the peg and his mouth in a smile. With a wink and a chuckle he was out the back door and off to the barn.

"That man," her mother said. "You'd think after twenty-eight years he wouldn't be such a flirt."

"You don't know how blessed you are, Mama." Not accustomed to contradicting her own mother, Martha stared into her teacup and tried desperately to blend in with the embroidered tablecloth.

"Wise words, I must say, dear."

The pity in her mother's voice soured Martha's tea. She did not need pity. She needed something to do.

Her mother brought two plates with eggs and biscuits, took her seat at the table and reached for Martha's hand.

"Thank You, Lord, for this family and our home and this food. Bless Caleb today and keep him in Your care. And please watch over us as we ride out to Whit's. Amen."

Expectation rushed the meal in spite of Martha's best efforts at nonchalance. The prospect of an entire morning with Haskell Jacobs had her more jittery than she cared to admit. Her mother made quick work of the breakfast dishes, and Martha wiped down the counter and brushed the table for crumbs. Bending to scoop them into the palm of her cradled right hand, she caught a movement through the back-door glass. Haskell stood next to the buckboard while her father adjusted Dolly's harness.

As dark and tall as her father, he seemed a match in body if not in spirit. He pulled his coat aside and reached into his vest pocket, revealing a long-barreled sidearm and holster. In the breaking sunlight, something metallic flashed on his vest. Her breath caught.

"What is it?" Martha's mother followed her gaze and then lifted her chin as if defying her husband's wishes. "Let me brush out your hair and we'll be on our way. The sooner we leave the better."

Martha sat sideways on the chair so the ladder back didn't interfere with her mother's work—and so she could watch for Haskell Jacobs to repeat his move. Could that bit of light have reflected from a badge? Is that why the man was so evasive?

The sight of the gun reopened a wound she thought had finally healed. It wasn't that guns were evil. Goodness, her father had several, and had seen to it that she and Whit knew how to properly care for and handle them.

But a gun had stolen her precious Joseph. What if gunplay erupted on the way to the ranch? What if another stray bullet took someone else's life—her mother's or her own? Her blood chilled.

"Let's not go, Mama." She felt her mother's tug at the bottom of the long braid and turned her head. "We don't have to go. There is no law that says we must ride out of town today. Let's wait until…until…I'm feeling better."

Her mother laid the brush on the table and picked up her satchel. "We can do this, Martha." She peered into the satchel's depths. "I have preserves for Whit, new linen for Livvy and peppermint sticks for the boys."

"But Mama, what if—"

"Martha, you can what-if your life away if you're not

careful. Come on." Her mother gathered her wrap and bonnet, and fairly ran out the back door. Martha had no bonnet and that silly hat she'd worn on the train was upstairs. Besides, it did nothing to keep the sun off her face.

She lifted an old garden hat from the pegs by the door. Better to hide beneath the wide brim than freckle her nose on the way, for the sun had indeed pushed through the clouds and promised to shine on them today.

Haskell watched Mrs. Hutton march to the buckboard and accept her husband's help to the seat. Martha followed like a flitting bird, less dignified and trying desperately to hide beneath a wide-brim straw hat. He sucked in the side of his mouth to keep from laughing.

The parson helped his daughter, too, holding her by the waist as she climbed into the seat. Satisfied that the women were comfortable, Haskell returned to Cache at the fence, grabbed the reins and swung up. He tipped his hat to Hutton and pulled up beside the man's wife.

"I'll follow you out of town, then come alongside once we make the turn at Soda Point."

Mrs. Hutton gathered the ribbons. "That will be quite acceptable." She snapped the leather on the mare's rump and the wagon jerked ahead. He got the distinct impression that he was not welcome on the outing.

So be it. The less obliged he'd be to make small talk with two women.

He glanced back. Hutton leaned against the corral, arms folded at his chest, a smile plastered on his face.

Haskell's hands started to sweat. The same way they always did just before he rousted an outlaw.

They rode past the paint shop, a bookstore, a drugstore. The city bakery, a meat market, millinery, post office and several clothing and dry goods establishments. Cañon had everything a larger city offered, except the crowds and smell of too many people in one place. Every morning since he'd arrived, he'd noticed the clear air, clearer even than Denver.

At Soda Point they followed the road around the end of the hogbacks, as locals called the jagged ridge. He heeled Cache into a quick trot and pulled up beside the women.

Not that he expected—or wanted—conversation, but he was a man of his word.

Neither looked his way. He might as well not be there at all.

A few miles on at the next bend, the women turned off on a road to the northeast that Haskell assumed led to the ranch. Immediately Cache stiffened beneath him and shot his ears forward to the water-gouged roadbed. The mare, Dolly, jerked to a stop, screamed as she reared in the harness and shied off the road. Haskell kicked Cache ahead and reached for the mare's bridle. The wagon wheels rolled into a deep crevice and the wagon pitched to the right, threatening to toss its passengers and flip the crazed horse.

Haskell scanned the ground. He pulled his .45 and with one shot separated the coiled body from a rattler's fang-bared head.

The women screamed, Cache danced backward and the harnessed mare rolled her eyes white with fear as she strained against the unyielding buckboard.

"Jump to the road!" Haskell holstered his gun.

Mrs. Hutton stared at him with her mouth open.

"Jump or break your neck when the wagon rolls."

She reached back for Martha who was clinging to the tipped seat with one hand.

"Alone!" He reined Cache clear of the spot where Mrs. Hutton should land. "Jump alone. I'll get Martha."

With a last, desperate prayer of a look, she jumped and pitched forward onto her hands and face with a grunt.

Haskell swung his leg over and leapt from the off side

of his horse. He helped her to her feet and turned back to the groaning wagon. Both left wheels cleared the ground. "Jump, Martha. I'll catch you."

He gripped the front wheel with one hand and held the other out to the white-faced woman with her arm in a sling.

She didn't move.

Chapter 9

Time slowed as Haskell's face pleaded with Martha to let him save her. Again. His voice she could not hear, for her hammering heart sounded over and over in her ears: "We should not have come."

She looked at his lips. "I'll catch you," they mouthed. What choice did she have?

She stood and gathered her skirt as high as possible, considering dignity to be of less value than one's life. The wagon shimmied and groaned. She stepped to the edge and pushed off into Haskell Jacobs's waiting arms.

He crushed her against his chest, her feet off the ground, her slinged arm pressed between them and the other around his neck. If he didn't let her go, she would faint for lack of air.

"I've got you, I've got you," he whispered against her hair. "You're safe now."

The urgency in his voice and the pounding of his heart made her question who had been the more frightened.

"Marti!"

Her mother's voice brought Martha's head up and she looked into blue depths deeper than the last time she'd been so close to them. She squirmed against him, and when he failed to take notice, she pushed with her free hand.

"Please put me down. My mother is hurt."

As if startled by her voice, he let her go and stepped back. Martha spun toward her mother and the motion unbalanced her. A steely grip fastened onto her left elbow and a deep voice brushed her ear. "Maybe you should sit and let me look after her."

Martha jerked her arm away, instantly shamed by the ungrateful response. But her mother was hurt. They should not have come. When would people listen to her and take her seriously?

She glanced up as the shade dropped over Haskell's eyes.

"Thank you," she said, "but I'll be fine." Testing her legs and finding them sound, she hurried to where her mother sat in the road.

Kneeling, she pushed back the bonnet to get a better look at a swelling, graveled rash.

"Ow!" Her mother jerked and knocked Martha's hand away.

"Can you stand, Mama?" Anger, fear and relief braided a tight rope around Martha's insides. She didn't know whether to laugh, scream or cry, but she helped her torn and dusty mother to her feet. Haskell stood beside the wagon as if afraid to approach.

So much for gallant.

"I hurt my ankle," her mother said.

Together they hobbled to the roadside where her mother leaned against a large boulder and pulled her bonnet on. "I don't think I can walk the rest of the way."

Martha looked at Haskell as if he had the answer to all their problems and then chided herself for doing so. She helped her mother into a sitting position and elevated her right foot on the rock. "We'll figure something out," she said, patting her mother's hand as if Martha were the parent and her mother the child.

Straightening, she wiped her face and flipped her braid behind her shoulder. Then she walked to the wagon that leaned precariously on two wheels and looked it over.

"We can pull it upright," she told Haskell who had begun unharnessing the mare.

"No, we can't."

Martha planted her free hand on her hip. Men were absolutely mulish at times. "And why not? We can leverage enough weight between the two of us to right it."

He stopped his fiddling, looked her up and down in a most forward way and then snorted. "Right."

If he had been closer, she would have slapped him.

"Why do you want to exert all that energy for nothing?"

Did she have to sketch it out for him? "So we can ride on to the ranch, of course."

He went back to fighting the twisted leather and didn't look at her at all. She wasn't sure which was worse: his ogling or his disregard.

"Look at the front axle." He pulled a knife from his boot and deftly sliced through the trace.

She looked.

The wood had splintered just inside the right wheel. They wouldn't be taking the buckboard anywhere.

Martha turned away and stared up at the cedar-speckled hills. Patches of red rock pocked the landscape and a hawk screeched above them. The sky was terrifyingly blue, burned clear of every cloud by a bold, autumn sun. She reached for her hat. It was gone.

"You and your mother will ride the horses."

The voice was so near that she whirled into it and nearly into Haskell. He'd approached her without a sound, like a bandit. Like the snake that had suddenly been there. She shuddered.

But a snake didn't wear a look so full of longing that she wanted to clutch it to her breast. She met his gaze without deferment. He stepped closer, smelling of sweat and dust and horses. His coat had been tossed aside and the star on his vest lay flat and dull with his back to the sun.

"Can you ride?" His eyes tore away any possibility of pretense on her part. There was no place to hide, no words to shield her from his scrutiny.

"Yes. It's been a while, but yes. So can Mama."

"Good. I'll put you on Cache. You can trust him. And your mother will be more comfortable on her own horse. She'll be bareback, but she has two good arms."

Again Martha's foolishness came home to roost and she flexed her right hand against the stiffness. "What about you?"

"I have two good legs." A near smile pulled at his mouth, but he strode away to her mother.

Martha followed.

"Do you think you can ride the mare, Mrs. Hutton?" He knelt on one knee before her, like a knight before a lady. The image shocked Martha, but she pushed it aside and listened for her mother's reply.

"Dolly? Oh, yes, I believe I can. I raised her. If I can't ride her, I'm a poor excuse for a horseman's wife." She stood, favoring her right ankle, and brushed dirt from her torn skirt and sleeves. "If you'll help me get on her." Raising her chin with a characteristic air of determination, she limped toward the horse now freed from the dead wagon but still quivering from the accident.

Haskell had cut the reins shorter and knotted them for easier handling. Her mother stood close to the mare, stroking its neck and calming the animal with soft murmurs. Haskell handed her the reins, she nodded her acceptance and with his hands around her waist he hefted her up. She threw her right leg over and perched atop the old yellow horse as if she did it every day.

Martha nearly cheered.

Then he led Cache to where she waited, looped the reins over the horse's head and linked his fingers together like a stirrup.

"Grab the horn, step into my hands with your left foot and I'll lift you high enough to throw your leg over."

His mention of her limbs brought a blush to her face, but this was no time for proprieties. If it were not for Haskell Jacobs, she and her mother would be walking.

A sudden truth speared her. Were it not for Haskell Jacobs, she and her mother could be dead beneath an overturned wagon.

"Well?" He looked up from his stooped position, and his expression betrayed impatience with her dawdling.

"Yes, thank you. I shall do just that." She hiked her skirt, stepped into his joined hands and had barely a moment to grab the saddle horn before she shot into the air above the horse. She swung her leg over and landed unceremoniously in the seat. Taking a deep breath, she felt for the stirrups with her toes.

"If you will allow me," he said with that near smile, "I will set the stirrups for you."

Burning with embarrassment, she hiked her skirt again and bent her leg at the knee. Haskell quickly shortened the leather straps and then repeated the process on the other side.

"You are a mite shorter than I am," he said as if he appreciated it.

"Mr. Jacobs." Martha's mother reined the mare around. "I had a satchel with me on the seat. Is there any way…?"

Haskell's jaw flexed. Her mother asked too much, but Martha kept her thoughts to herself. Let the knight prove just how gallant he could be.

He adjusted his hat and walked around the back of the forlorn wagon. It teetered at the top of a steep draw, and Martha feared the slightest movement might send it rolling down the embankment. It wasn't worth a few jars of preserves—or Haskell's life. Anyone's life, she corrected, as if her feelings were on display.

For several moments Martha and her mother sat silently waiting for Haskell's return. Martha strained her ears for any indication of his success or hazard, but only the wheeling hawk pierced the hot silence, along with an occasional chirp from a ground squirrel and the trickle of loose rocks tumbling down the ravine. She wiped her face and neck with the hem of her skirt.

Finally he came up at the wagon's front end, balancing his climb with one hand and holding the satchel in the other. The sight of his dusty clothes, sweat-soaked shirt, and that satchel must have weakened her mother's reserve, for she nearly fawned over the man as he lifted the battered bag.

"Oh, Mr. Jacobs, you are so kind." She reached for the satchel. "Thank you for your help. I so appreciate—"

"You can't ride and carry this, too." He walked to Cache and tied the bag to the saddle with leather thongs that hung from the fork. His armor may not be shining—not even his star shone—but he was definitely winning the joust with her mother.

Small talk had been Haskell's chief concern. He grunted.

Yes, there were more reasonable ways to get to the ranch. Martha could ride behind her mother, but she had only one good arm to hold on with. The same reason he had for not pulling her up behind him on Cache. And he did not ride behind a woman. Which meant he walked.

From his conversation this morning with the parson, he guessed they were about four miles from the ranch. He'd hoofed it farther and in worse conditions.

At least he had a hat. He looked over his shoulder to Martha bringing up the rear. Her face was reddening but she rode well enough. Her mother was in obvious discomfort with her swollen ankle dangling low, but at least it bore no weight.

His presence had turned out to be rather providential after all. What else could account for his being nearby with a gun when the women needed one most?

Providence. A word that didn't often visit his thoughts. He kicked a stone from the path.

He knew what the Good Book said about man being alone and had sure enough felt the pain of it since the widow stepped off the train. If he ever prayed again, he'd ask about the parson's daughter.

From the position of the sun, it was dead noon or thereabouts as they trudged into the ranch yard. Two young boys and a black-and-white dog came running to greet them, the dog more cautious than the boys.

Its bark must have called an alarm, for a fair-haired woman appeared round back of the long, low ranch house, a basket on her arm and a hand shading her eyes. When she recognized the lead in their procession, she dropped the basket and came running.

"Annie! Whatever happened? Are you all right?"

The mare tossed her head as Mrs. Hutton reined her to a stop. The younger woman grabbed the headstall and pegged Haskell with a blistering glare.

"Oh, Livvy." Mrs. Hutton reached over the mare's neck. "It's so good to see you, but we hadn't intended to come dragging in like this." She turned to Haskell with an expectant look. "Would you be so kind as to help me down?"

If Martha aged as well as her mother, she'd still be a fine-looking woman in twenty years. Haskell shelved the thought and slid Mrs. Hutton from the mare's back. Livvy came round to catch her mother-in-law's arm across her shoulder.

"Let's get you inside with a glass of lemonade and you must tell me what happened. Did you fall? Look at your skirt—it's torn, and oh—your head."

She fussed and bustled and Haskell left her to it. He

turned to see Martha attempting to dismount and made it to her just as she lost her balance. She landed in his arms rather than in the dirt. He suspected her dignity took more of a beating than her backside would have, and he bit his cheek to squelch a chuckle.

"Oh," she blurted out. "Thank you." Righting herself and brushing at her dusty clothes, she met his eyes again with that bold, unabashed gaze that weakened his knees.

"What would we ever have done without you?"

What would he do the rest of his life without her?

The words nearly fell out of his mouth.

"You must be parched. Please, come inside for some lemonade." She touched his arm.

"I will after I see to the horses."

The two youngsters chose that moment to offer their assistance and as they approached, the dog joined the ruckus and sniffed about Haskell's boots and trousers.

"We'll help, mister. We can each take a horse."

"You must be Whit and Livvy's boys," Martha said, as she'd never met them.

Two grins popped out beneath their blue eyes, a reflection of their mother's. The dark hair must have come from Whit.

"You kinda look like Grandma," said one.

"But younger," said the other, more diplomatic of the two.

Unoffended, Martha spread her good arm. "Come give your aunt Martha a hug, boys. And tell me who is who."

A knot in Haskell's gut tightened.

The boys obliged.

"I'm Cale."

"And I'm Hugh. I'm the oldest."

"Just by a minute."

Martha embraced each in turn and then tousled their hair. Haskell's children might look like that if he ever had any. But that required a wife and right now he was looking at the likeliest prospect he'd ever met.

Squirming in their aunt's affection, they politely ended the encounter and turned to Haskell.

"Our pa taught us everything there is to know 'bout horses," said one.

"That's right," said the other. "Ask us anything."

Rubbing his jaw, he feigned consideration and then posed his query. "Which eat more, black horses or white horses?"

Puzzled, the youngsters discussed it between themselves.

"Seems as we don't rightly know," the first one said.

"Well, now. I thought you knew everything."

One kicked the dirt and the other stuck his chest out at the challenge.

Chuckling, Haskell made them an offer. "If you'll rub down our mounts, give them water and turn them out in that pasture over there, I'll tell you how to find the answer."

They each grabbed a horse's reins and were on their way before one thought to yell back, "Thanks, mister."

Maybe if he had a lick o' luck, they'd someday call him "uncle."

"Now you have no excuse." Fatigue edged Martha's voice as she tugged at his arm. Her touch shot through him like a fire. "Come in the house, have something to drink and rest. You must be weary from that long dusty walk."

Was this the same woman who had scorned him three short days ago from the blue velvet settee in the parsonage?

Or was this the woman he longed to take in his arms and into his heart and never let go?

Chapter 10

A covered porch had been added to the front of the ranch house, but when Haskell opened the heavy front door for Martha, it still led directly into the old dining room. She withdrew her hand from his arm and stepped through time to Whit and Livvy's wedding in that very room. A new carpet covered the floor, setting off the same elegant furniture Livvy's grandmother had brought from England. A crystal vase on the dining table held a fistful of bright sunflowers, and their upright, happy faces momentarily eased Martha's weariness.

Haskell removed his hat and waited, observing her without watching. He did that a lot, a trait she now assumed had to do with his work.

Voices drew her to the kitchen where Livvy tended her mother, a bare foot resting in a basin of water. Annie's face colored at Haskell's approach and she lowered her skirt around the basin.

If Martha were not so worn out, she'd mention her mother's undying sense of propriety. But the woman had borne enough today, and it was all Martha could do to drop into the nearest chair.

Livvy squeezed out a cloth and pressed it to her mother-in-law's brow, chattering like an old maid on Sunday morning. She glanced up as Martha joined them and reached for her hand.

"Oh, Marti, I didn't mean to ignore you." She drew

back, eyeing first one woman and then the other. "You two look like you had a time of it getting here." She glared at Haskell who stood apart and aloof.

Defensiveness fired in Martha's breast, a need to inform Livvy that Haskell was not the cause of their unkempt condition but the savior of their lives. She gestured toward him but avoided his eyes. They had power to open the door of her affections.

"Livvy, this is Mr. Haskell Jacobs, a friend of my father."

In spite of the gun he carried—thank God he carried it today—he seemed less intimidating than before, less daunting. His stony expression remained in place, but he jerked his quick nod and worked the brim of his hat with one hand.

Martha flipped her braid behind her shoulder. "Haskell, this is my brother's wife, Livvy."

"Nice to make your acquaintance, ma'am."

A bowl of lemons sat on the counter next to a wooden press—not yet the refreshing drink she expected. Martha went to the sink where she filled a cup with cool water and handed it to Haskell. He'd parch to death if he had to wait for the lemonade.

She felt the burn of his eyes on her face as he took the cup, careful not to touch her fingers in the process. She risked a glance and confirmed her instincts.

"Thank the Lord, Mr. Jacobs was with us today." Martha's mother appraised him from a more relaxed and dignified position, but true appreciation shone in her eyes.

"What happened?" Livvy handed the damp rag to Martha. "Can you do this while I get the sugar water off the stove?"

Her mother snatched the cloth. "I am perfectly capable of washing my own face."

Livvy set the syrupy mixture aside and brought the

bowl of lemons to the table with a pitcher, knife and press. "Did you meet with outlaws on the road to the ranch?"

"Excuse me, Mrs. Hutton?" All three women looked at Haskell.

He cleared his throat. "That is, Miss Livvy—is Whit about?"

She sliced a lemon in two, clamped half into the wooden press and held it over the pitcher. "He must be out with the cattle or he would have come up at all the commotion." She stopped and turned with a pensive look. "If you don't mind riding out, you might find him down at the lower corrals. Just head for the rimrock east of here and watch for the windmill. You can't miss it."

He donned his hat. "Thank you, ma'am." He slid a look to Martha and all her insides backed up against her spine. She swallowed hard and accepted his empty cup. He jerked another quick nod and that near smile tipped one side of his mouth.

Now she was noticing his mouth.

"Let me help you with that lemonade, Livvy." She set down the cup and dragged the bowl and knife toward her as the front door clicked shut.

The knife blade slammed against the wooden table and lemon juice squirted her mother.

"Martha—use the board or you'll slice right through Livvy's table." She rubbed her eyes with the damp rag and sloshed her foot in the pan. Hiking her skirt above her knee, she leaned over to assess the damage.

"Swelling's gone down some."

"But it should be raised," Livvy put in. "Since the men are all gone, let's get your foot higher." She lifted the basin to a low stool beneath the table and helped Annie transfer her foot. "Pop used this stool to rest his bad leg. Good thing I kept it."

Martha halved three more lemons and picked up the

press but couldn't manage it with just one hand. "What have you done with the old Overton place Whit bought before you were married? Did he ever finish the cabin?"

Livvy fetched the sugar water and dumped it in the pitcher. "Oh, yes. But since we moved back here, he just uses it as a branding camp. We didn't live there long, not after Pop got so crippled up and needed us closer."

"Give me a spoon," Martha's mother said. "I can at least stir while I'm sitting here like an invalid."

"It's so good to have you both here." Livvy handed her a long wooden spoon and took the press from Martha. "I'm just so surprised, that's all. I didn't know you were coming back to Cañon, Marti, though it seems like the natural thing to do." Her blue eyes rested on Martha with compassion, and she lowered her voice from its cheerful pitch. "I was so shocked to hear about Joseph."

Martha inhaled deeply, hoping to head off the old pain. "Thank you. I wanted to finish the school term and then I lingered in St. Louis for the summer. Uncertain, I suppose." She sighed and adjusted her sling, disgusted with its limitations. Tentatively, she lifted the knot over her head and pulled the cloth from her right arm. She hunched her shoulder and straightened her elbow.

Her mother watched with concern. "How does it feel?"

"Tight," Martha said. "Like I haven't used it in a few days."

"Well, you haven't. And you probably want to keep it in that sling until we get home this evening."

Martha tensed at the mother-hen response, but she had no chance to reply.

"How long have you known Haskell Jacobs?" Livvy squeezed another lemon into the pitcher.

Martha glanced at her mother who merely regarded her with a stoic expression and kept stirring.

She took another deep breath, intent on hiding the little flame that stirred in her belly at mention of his name. "Just a few days." Since she stepped off the train and into his scrutiny.

"Well, I think he's taken with you."

Martha stared. "What makes you say that?"

"He looks at you as if the sun and moon and all the stars rose in your face."

The heat rose, that was for certain, as did Martha before walking to the kitchen door and opening it to the clear mountain air. She pushed at her mussed hair with both hands. How could she ache for Joseph with one breath and have her heart race for another man in the next?

"I don't mean to say he's besotted with you. More like watchful. Protective, as if trying to anticipate your moves. But adoration is definitely lurking."

Her mother laughed nervously. "It's a bit early for that. We've known Mr. Jacobs such a short while. Though I must say, he is quite gentlemanly, in spite of his attire. Which reminds me—" She scooted her chair around. "Martha, did you bring in my satchel?"

"No, I left it on the saddle. I'll get it for you." Anything to escape Livvy's speculation on Haskell Jacobs's unsettling observation.

From the way the approaching rider sat the saddle, Haskell pegged him as the son of Caleb Hutton.

The cowboy pulled up and dismounted, eyeing him with caution. "You lookin' for someone?"

Haskell extended his hand. "Haskell Jacobs, Colorado Ranger. Pastor Hutton suggested I see his son, Whit, about a matter. I accompanied the pastor's wife and daughter here today. I take it you're Whit?"

The man scanned the empty yard, the pasture, pausing on the boys stroking two strange horses.

Haskell read the question. "A rattler spooked the mare.

The wagon's tipped at a deep gully just after the turnoff. Broke the front axle. Mrs. Hutton and her daughter rode my horse and the wagon mare the rest of the way here."

At that, the cowboy swept Haskell's dust-covered clothing with a quick appraisal. "Let's see what I've got in the barn in the way of an axle and you can tell me why my father sent you."

One way to answer a direct question.

From the corner of his eye, Haskell caught Martha in the shade of the ranch house. Eavesdropping on what her brother might say about Tad Overton? Disappointment wedged itself between his hopes and better judgment. He followed Whit to the barn.

"Was the snake coiled or sunnin' itself?" Whit dropped his horse's reins at the corral, unsaddled it and draped his rig over the top rail.

"Coiled."

Whit stepped into a tack room just inside the barn door, came back with a brush and glanced at Haskell's sidearm. "I take it you solved the problem."

"Changed its mind."

Whit snorted. "Best solution I know of."

The twins were pulling grass and feeding it to the horses. Whit brushed his mount and turned it out. "Nice gray."

"Thanks." Haskell couldn't agree more. Cache was the closest thing he had to a friend, besides the captain. The realization made him feel old and lonely. "He's sound and true."

Whit took his rig to the tack room, and they walked the brief alleyway to an open area where a buckboard sat between two wide doors on either side of the barn. Haskell paused at the last stall and glanced back at the ranch house. Martha was nearly to the barn.

"So what does my father think I know?" Whit set a

bucket of axle grease in the buckboard and pulled a spare axle away from a pile of timber against the wall. Haskell hurried around to get the opposite end, and they hefted it into the wagon.

"I'm trailing a horse thief rumored to be holed up in the area. Your father thinks there's a possibility that he could be the son of Doc Mason's nurse."

The remark hitched the cowboy's otherwise smooth and easy movements, and his expression hardened. Evidently, he didn't think kindly of Tad Overton.

Whit took his hat off and wiped the sweat from his head with his sleeve. "More than a possibility. He was through a couple of days ago with a string of four horses. Tried to sell 'em to me, but the freshly run brands told me they weren't his to sell." He muttered something under his breath. "Like he thought I wouldn't notice."

"How well do you know him?" Haskell said.

Whit made a sound in his throat. "Better than I care to."

"Do you know which way he headed?"

The hat landed hard. "West, toward Texas Creek."

"How far is that?"

"Half a day's ride." Whit eyed him "From town, not here. You could make it quicker from the ranch."

"Sounds like you wouldn't mind seeing him caught."

Whit snorted. "I couldn't just take off and ride into town to tell the sheriff. Overton's been a no-account all his life. Left his ma in the lurch and got himself shot during the train wars, abandoned a good dog when it was a defenseless pup and now he's stealin' horses. Yeah, I'd like to see him get his due."

"I understand he fancied your sister at one time." What that had to do with Haskell's manhunt he was unwilling to admit.

Like a bullet, Whit's look burned through him. "Fuel for the fire." He grabbed a heavy hammer and tossed in the wagon. "Let me know if you need help bringing him in, and I'll ride with you."

Haskell appreciated the cowboy's willingness, but he didn't need a gut-driven vigilante shooting his suspect. "I'll keep that in mind."

A clearing throat turned both their heads to the alleyway. Martha stood with hands clasped before her—minus the sling—and her chin reaching for the rafters. "Excuse me, but have either of you seen my mother's satchel? You remember, Mr. Jacobs. You tied it to your saddle as we were leaving the wagon."

Mr. Jacobs. She'd heard enough to learn his intentions but not enough to know the intention of his heart.

"Your nephews may know its whereabouts. I asked them to care for the horses."

She turned with a sharp jerk of her head and the braid snapped like the tail of a bullwhip. Before he could reach her, the twins came running through the alleyway and nearly knocked her down in their hurry.

"Whoa, whoa, whoa!" She snagged each one and flinched when one boy hit the end of her right arm's reach.

He stepped forward. "What'd you boys do with the satchel that was tied to the saddle?"

The pair stopped wiggling and looked as if they didn't know what he was talking about.

He nailed each one with a hard glare. "Where's the saddle?" If it was lying in the pasture it would take more than the presence of their father to prevent him from whipping them both.

One pointed sharply to the tack room and the other's mouth opened as if attached to the finger. "It's hanging on a rack in there. With all the other rigs."

His jaw relaxed. "Good work, men." He clapped one on the shoulder as he squeezed past the boy and Martha.

Giving his eyes time to adjust to the dim interior, he

pegged his saddle on the bottom rack, the satchel still attached and looking like it'd been dragged up the ravine again. He untied the leather thongs and brushed off the dirt. When he turned for the door, she stood at the threshold, her face a study in sculptured control.

And beauty.

She held out her hand. The chin remained aloft. "Thank you."

He wanted to explain, but he doubted she'd listen. He handed her the bag without letting go. His grip forced her to look at him and cold water could not have doused him more than her icy regard. He released the bag and she marched from the barn.

Whit joined him in the alleyway. "She heard us." He looked at Haskell. "Didn't she know what you were riding out here for?"

"She didn't even know I'm a ranger."

"That matters?"

Haskell broke from his personal thoughts and forced himself back to the issue at hand. "It could."

"I take it you don't know how her husband died."

Haskell cut him a sideways glance and then watched her stride toward the house.

"A stray bullet caught him in the head. Died right there in a St. Louis street. He was a preacher, too."

The news hit Haskell like the lead that dropped Martha's husband. Not only had she been the wife of a decent, God-fearing man, she was the widow of one brought down by a gun.

No wonder the sight of his Colt filled her eyes with terror.

He didn't have a chance.

Chapter 11

Hot tears clogged Martha's throat. So much for the gallant Mr. Jacobs. He was convinced Tad Overton was a horse thief and no doubt planned to shoot him down in the street the first chance he got.

How dare she give a gunman a second glance—lawman or not. She should have known better.

She burst through the kitchen door, dropped the satchel on the table and hurried through to the dining room, away from curious eyes. With no place to hide in her humiliation, she stepped inside the adjacent study, closed the door and leaned against it.

A man's study. The smell of leather and oiled wood filled the room, shooting fine pinpricks against her already aching sensibilities. She locked the door and turned the large desk chair to face the window overlooking distant bluffs and green pastures. Dropping onto the worn leather seat with a hiccup, she let the tears slip down her face unchecked.

Betrayal crawled in and curled up next to her heart.

She didn't cry for Tad. Her childish infatuation with him had dissolved years ago when she fell in love with Joseph. She didn't even cry for Joseph. He was with the God he loved, as her mother had said. The God *she* loved. But sometimes the Lord felt so distant, so in cahoots with every other man in her life, like her father who had turned Haskell Jacobs onto Tad's trail.

A few tears, she admitted, were for the tall ranger. What a fool she'd been to think something might grow between them.

She sniffed and wrapped her arms around her middle. She cried for herself, fully aware of pity's suffocating grip. Fishing in her skirt pocket for a hankie and finding none, she wiped her eyes with her sleeve, pulled up her petticoat hem and blew her nose. Her mother would have been appalled.

All she wanted was a loving marriage like her parents had. And children. Fresh tears burned and she coughed against the tightening in her chest.

At a knock on the door she flinched and her shoulder tightened with a sharp stab.

"Marti?"

Livvy. "Yes?" She cringed at the soggy edge to her voice.

"Are you all right?"

No, she was not all right. "Yes. I'm fine." The break in the last word ruined her prospects for taking up lying as a profession.

The doorknob rattled, then lay still in its place. "May I come in?"

Martha pulled her petticoat up again and pressed it to her face. Livvy was asking to come into a room in her own house. Humiliation flared. "Just a moment."

Taking a deep breath, she stood and smoothed her skirts. At the door, she turned the key and stepped back. Martha stiffened at Livvy's worried expression. They were so close in age, yet so far apart in wisdom and experience.

"Of course you may come in. This is your home. I apologize for locking the door."

Livvy stepped inside, shut the door and pulled Martha into her arms. The gesture drained every drop of resolve from Martha's body.

Groping inwardly for composure, she pulled away and held her sleeve against her eyes. Livvy took her other hand and pressed a hankie into it.

"Thank you." Martha's nose and head were so clogged with tears that she didn't recognize her own voice.

Livvy pulled a side chair to the end of the desk. "Come and sit," she said, leaving her grandfather's desk chair empty. "What is it that has you tied in such a knot?"

Martha walked to the window and stood for a long moment drinking in the expansive blue sky, verdant meadows and rocky bluffs. Such contrasting elements that balanced the scene rather than warring within it. So unlike her inner landscape.

With a wavering breath, she returned to the leather chair and faced her sister-in-law. Not long after Livvy and Whit married, Martha had left for school. She'd not had much chance to get to know her brother's wife and she steeled herself for an inquisition.

Instead, a kind smile settled in Livvy's eyes and she said nothing, and simply waited, unhurried and unflustered.

Martha sucked in a broken breath. "I have no life."

The declaration informed Martha herself as well as Livvy. She'd not faced it head-on, but as she sought to explain, she realized the depth of her problem.

"I have no husband, no children, no substance."

Livvy folded her hands on her apron and looked out the window over Martha's shoulder. Her yellow hair reminded Martha of Joseph's. They could have been siblings.

"I am not surprised you feel that way." Livvy's gaze took in the same ranch land that Martha had regarded. "When I first moved here, I was running away from the mundane life of a preacher's daughter entombed in a city. My heart longed for something else, I just didn't know what."

She looked at Martha. "Until I saw the ranch and your brother."

Martha huffed. "You knew Whit when we were all children."

"Not the Whit he became as a grown man."

Martha still considered him an overbearing big brother, though she'd tried to cut him free of that image.

"But it was more than that," Livvy continued. "I took care of Pop, fed the crew here, tended to the garden and chickens and canning and cooking. I had a sense of purpose." She returned her gaze to the window. "And I had your mother's encouragement to trust the Lord with my heart and stop trying to figure things out on my own."

Shame bent over Martha and breathed heavily down her neck. She'd not listened enough to her mother's counsel. Usually she bristled against it.

"I know you see her differently than I do." Livvy laughed. "I certainly don't view my own mother with the same regard, and for that I confess my sin. It's often difficult to see a parent's wisdom when you know them so well."

Martha's back eased, the tension in her shoulder lessened. Whit had made a good choice for a wife.

"But it is worse for you."

Martha locked her eyes on Livvy. Maybe she had judged too soon. She waited for the ax of accusation to fall.

"You have had a purpose and a life, as you put it, and lost it. No wonder you feel bereft."

Martha blinked hard. She had no more use for tears. They swelled her face, blurred her vision and did her no good.

"But never doubt that you have substance. I know what your mother would say—'Faith is the substance of things hoped for.' You have faith and you have hope. Therefore, you have substance."

Martha sat numbed by the simplicity with which her sister-in-law spoke. The verse she referenced had been one of Joseph's favorites. Why had it not come to mind since his death?

Haskell's head turned at the brilliant clang coming from the ranch house. He'd nearly forgotten the sound of a stirring call to dinner and envisioned the woman rounding the bar against the triangle. Little hope was left to paint in the face of Martha Hutton.

He and Whit had worked amicably for an hour, switching out a broken pole in the corral, laughing at the boys as they scattered hay in a mock brawl and then grumbled their way through raking it into a neat pile.

"If you ever change your mind about the Rangers, you'd do all right on a ranch." Whit leaned his shovel and the boys' rakes against the wall. "Might even hire you on myself. If you can rope from horseback, that is."

The younger man pushed up his hat up with his arm. A wide grin broke through a week-old beard. Haskell suspected Livvy would soon be after her husband with a straight razor.

Whit turned to his sons. "Go wash up. Don't keep your ma waiting."

"But Mr. Jacobs owes us for takin' care of his horses." One dark-haired youngster stood his ground and held a narrowed eye on Haskell.

"You're right." Haskell snagged his gun belt from a high nail, strapped it on, then rolled down his sleeves.

"And what might that be?" Whit said to the boys. "You're not takin' money for being hospitable."

"'Tain't money, Pa."

"It isn't." Whit hammered the words with a frown. "Your mother'll have my hide if she hears you talking like that."

Haskell sucked his cheek between his teeth and grabbed his hat.

"He said he'd tell us how to figure what kind of horse eats more—a black one or a white one."

Whit scrubbed his face and made a rough noise behind his hand.

Haskell squatted before the boys and looked one in the eye and then the other. "Count 'em."

Two dark brows tucked down in puzzlement and they turned to each other as if pulled by the same string.

"Count what?" said the narrow-eyed challenger.

"The horses. How many white ones, how many black ones?"

Light cracked in the blue eyes of the other boy and he let out a whoop. "Ha! You got us good." He hopped around on one foot and slapped his brother on the back. "Don't you see? If you got more white horses than black ones, the white ones eat more. And the other way round if you got more black horses."

Whit laughed, grabbed each boy by a shoulder and turned them toward the house. "Off with you. Dinner's waitin' and don't forget to wash."

The pair ran off, shoving each other like two unruly racehorses on the final stretch.

"Cale! Hugh!" Like a whip crack they stopped their antics and walked the rest of the way until they rounded the corner of the house and were out of sight. A high-pitched "Hey!" rolled across the yard to the barn and Whit shook his head.

"They're good boys," Haskell said, heading for the house.

"But they're a bucket full o' bobcat, I tell you what." The disclaimer did nothing to dim the pride in the young father's eyes. Haskell tasted envy on his tongue. A bitter and unpleasant flavor.

Nearly as unpleasant as dinner with Martha sitting feet away and miles apart. She refused to meet his eye, yet was a lively conversationalist with everyone else. It was as if he didn't exist, and she made it clear that she wished it were so.

He scooted back from the dining room table. "Thank you, ma'am." He nodded to Livvy who responded with a warm smile.

"You are quite welcome, Mr. Jacobs."

To Mrs. Hutton, he added, "Whit's offered us the use of his buckboard. I'll be saddling up so we can get on the road and have your wagon repaired before dark."

"I understand, Mr. Jacobs. Martha and I will help clear things away and be right out."

If he had his way, he'd be taking Martha Hutton out to the porch and clearing things away between the two of them. He was too old for games and he wasn't about to chase her like a spring calf. Either she'd have him or she wouldn't. And the sooner he found out what was wrong, the better.

The axle was an easy fix between the men, and within a couple of hours, Haskell was driving to Cañon City, seated on the bench next to Mrs. Hutton. Martha rode Cache, who had decided to show his gentle side, and Whit was driving his wagon home with two youngsters in the back, as full of boyish pranks as Haskell had ever seen. He chuckled to himself and the sound drew Mrs. Hutton's attention.

"Do you find humor in this situation, Mr. Jacobs?"

The woman's voice so resembled her daughter's that he cut a sideways glance to banish his doubts. Martha still rode next to the wagon with a stiff back and a stiffer jaw. She'd regret it come morning.

"Only in the boys, ma'am. They are quite a pair."

At the mention of her grandsons, the woman's formal attitude eased and she sent him a beaming smile. "Aren't they? Oh, but they are so like their father when he was that age. Full of vinegar yet with little hearts of gold."

Martha snorted.

Annie took to studying her hands, and Haskell couldn't see past the sides of her bonnet. Something intangible shot between the two women. An unspoken regret. He skirted that badger hole and gave the reins a light slap as the yellow mare turned onto the main road.

By the time they pulled up to the parsonage, he wished he'd eaten more at dinner. Lights had still shone from the hotel dining room as they passed the St. Cloud, and he hoped they'd have something left after he unhitched the wagon and bid the Huttons good evening.

A saddled horse stood tied to the corral. He reined in the mare and the preacher bounded down the back porch steps.

"Ten minutes more and I was coming to find you." His worried gaze took in first his wife and then his daughter seated atop Cache.

"What a day," Annie said as she reached for her husband's shoulders and allowed him to lift her from the wagon. "We have quite a story to tell you, but let's get supper on the table first. Help me inside, dear. I've sprained my ankle and am not quite my quick-footed self."

Haskell caught the parson's suspicious look. He'd talk to the man later, after the womenfolk gave him their rendition of the day.

Looping the reins around the brake handle, he jumped down and offered his hand to Martha.

"Thank you, but I can dismount a horse, Mr. Jacobs." If her chin jutted any higher she'd drown come the next rainstorm.

Considering himself an all-or-nothing sort, he linked one arm around her waist and dragged her from the saddle. She'd stomp into the house without a word if he set her down, so he caught her under the legs with his other arm and made no move to take her inside.

She had instinctively circled his neck with both arms and he liked it. She sucked in a breath and her heart fluttered against his chest like a bird in a hunter's hand.

"Set me down this instant."

If she screamed, he was done for, but her demands contradicted her actions. Both arms remained round his neck. Which signal did he act on—her words or her gestures?

"We need to talk."

She blinked but held his eyes in a bold challenge. "About what, Mr. Jacobs?"

"About you calling me Haskell, among other things."

She relaxed a hair.

"Very well, *Haskell*. Kindly set me down."

The edge she added to his name confirmed that she'd bolt the minute her feet hit the ground. The warmth of her body seeped into his, melding them together. He intended to keep it that way for as long as possible.

"Do you promise not to run off?"

She looked away. "Yes."

"You're lying."

She went rigid again and knifed him with a cold glare. He wanted to laugh aloud, swing her around in his arms and feel her lips against his. Instead, he bounced her up as if to drop her and she gasped again and tightened her grip, tucking her head against his shoulder.

Much more and he *would* taste those lips. Instead, he dragged reason to the surface and laid out the facts.

"Number one—I am not going to drop you."

She raised her head and looked straight into his eyes.

"Number two—I am not your enemy."

Her chin lifted a notch.

"Number three—When we arrived at the ranch you

were sweet as molasses and when we left you were cold as stone."

She swallowed hard, an act that drew his eyes to her slender throat.

"Why?"

Her arms relaxed but she didn't let go and addressed her comment to her father's horse tied to the corral. "Why what?"

He bounced her and her head jerked back to face him.

"Look at me and ask me that."

Twins as close as her nephews shouted from her dark eyes—one anger and the other fear. The first he expected, the second set him back. He lowered his voice.

"You have nothing to fear from me, Martha."

"Really? You are holding me against my will and yet you say I have nothing to fear? Were I to scream, my father and all our neighbors would be out here in a heartbeat ready to lynch you from the nearest tree."

"Then scream if you're truly afraid."

She hesitated and his heart stopped.

At last she let out a defeated sigh. "Fine. I won't scream."

His arms ached, more from wrestling earlier with the upturned wagon than from holding her small, warm body. "Promise me you won't run away and I'll let you down."

She nodded.

He couldn't hold her all night, as much as he wanted to, so he lowered her feet, keeping one arm around her waist. She stood against him, her hands resting on his chest. Had she forgotten or did she want them there?

She looked up at him. "Why what?" The edge had softened, the tone deepened.

"Why did you distance yourself when we left the ranch—no—before that. At dinner. You had a word for everyone but me."

Her dark eyes searched his. "Why do you care if I spoke to you or not?"

He let go of her waist. "You answer my question first and then I will answer yours."

Her hands slipped away and the sensation left him feeling abandoned. She clasped her fingers and dropped her gaze. "I overheard you speaking to Whit in the barn about Tad Overton."

Though he already knew about their past, her admission twisted a knot of jealousy inside him. "Are you still fond of him?"

A small laugh escaped her lips and she shook her head. "That was many years ago and I was a child. I haven't even seen him since my return. But I don't want to see him—shot."

Her hand flew to her mouth and the two dark pools welled.

He reached for her other hand and held it between both of his. "Do you suspect he's a horse thief? Is that why you think I'd shoot him?"

She did not pull away but lowered her free hand to her stomach. He leaned nearer.

"I've seen a man die from a gunshot wound. I don't care to see another." Her small hand stiffened in his. "Now you must answer my question."

Chapter 12

Haskell linked his fingers with hers and Martha found herself responding. It was too easy to yield to his strength, to be swept up in his encompassing gaze. Three times he had held her, but this time not from necessity. Though she'd insisted her set her down out of propriety, she had felt safe in his arms, protected. More so than she had in months.

It was as if he knew. Had Whit told him about Joseph? Why had he thought she was fond of Tad? How much did he know?

As doubt and mistrust hefted themselves into a formidable wall, Haskell raised her fingers to his lips and held them there. His warmth invaded her. His chin was rough with a day-old beard, and she thought to lay her hand against his face.

Instead, he pressed it to his chest. His heartbeat pounded into her hand and down her arm until it mingled with her own.

"I care about you, Martha Hutton. I care that you talk to me, smile across the table at me like you do for others. I want to hear your voice and your dreams and—"

He stopped, startled by his own words, it seemed. Her temples pulsed and she grappled to maintain clarity of thought. Was Haskell Jacobs declaring himself to her?

Releasing her hand, he stepped back. "I apologize. I had no right to force myself upon you in such a manner."

She wrapped her arms about her middle, suddenly

chilled without his touch. The back door opened and her father stepped out. "Supper's on, you two. Best hurry before it's gone."

Haskell reset his hat. "I'll unhitch the wagon, settle your horse for the night and be on my way."

Did she dare ask him to stay? She'd done so once before and regretted it. But this time she feared she'd regret *not* asking him. *Make a fresh start,* her mother had said. Oh, if she could just sort out her thoughts.

The jangling harness broke through her confusion.

"Stay."

He turned his head toward her, his face shadowed. Martha held her breath. The quick jerk of his chin served as reply, and he finished unhitching the mare.

She looked around as if waking from a dream. The sun had long since set and night was creeping up against the house and barn. She gathered her skirts and took the back steps with care. Her heart raced as if she'd run all the way from the ranch. At the door she turned. Haskell looped his horse's reins on the corral, then unsaddled her father's horse and led it into the barn.

I care about you, Martha Hutton. So did her mother and father and grandmother. Did he mean what she hoped he meant?

She curved her fingers at her lips, the way he had held them against his own. Something stirred in her breast, broke through a stony sheath and spread delicate wings.

Livvy had stated the obvious. Yes, Martha had hopes. She just hadn't expected them to materialize in the form of a Colorado Ranger hunting the boy she'd once cared for.

With a twist of the doorknob, she stepped into the welcoming atmosphere of the parsonage. Her parents' affection for each other laced the room like a tangible thread. It had held her and her brother firmly to the family fabric in their childhood.

Tad had just the opposite—a gaping hole. His father's death embittered his mother, and he had no one to teach him how to be a loving, helpful son. He had chosen the wrong path through the hard place of loss.

Choice.

Her father read at the table and glanced up as she moved past. She washed her hands at the sink and dried them on a dish towel. Of all the things she'd had no control over in her life, she still had the power to choose her response to those inequities.

She peeked at her father. How often she'd chosen to resent his involvement, his *interference,* she had called it.

At the stove her mother leaned heavily to her left, favoring her right ankle. *Make a fresh start.* Even by not choosing, one chose a path: a barren desert place or pastures full and green, like those at the ranch.

Martha pressed her mother's arms from behind, brushed her cheek with a quick kiss and shooed her away. "Go sit and put that foot up. You know what Livvy said."

Her mother groused but retreated to her chair at the table where her husband lifted her foot into his lap, much to her distress. Martha turned away from the intimate scene. What if Haskell walked in on such a display?

When he opened the door, her mother nearly turned her chair over. To no avail she tried to free her foot from a husband who took too much delight in her discomfort. His eyes sparkled in the warm lamplight, but he conceded by scooting closer to the table, hiding her foot beneath the cloth.

Haskell halted and shot Martha a look, his hand suspended above his hat on the way to remove it.

"Please, come in," she said, failing to keep the laughter from her voice. Her parents were as lively as her nephews and always had been. She glanced sideways at Haskell and shivered at the memory of his earlier threat to drop her.

Had he been playing? Heat climbed the back of her neck for even considering such an intimate question.

She hurried to the pie safe for two vinegar pies. In-between pies, the family had always called them, made prior to the apple harvest.

Their Arkansas Black trees were heavy with fruit, but not enough for the winter, not with her father's sweet tooth and her mother's fame for apple butter.

Four place settings already topped the table, and Martha added the pies and a tureen of leftover soup that might stretch among them. Another parental trait—making do with what they had and sharing even that with outsiders.

Somehow, there was always enough.

Haskell filled the room with his hesitation, no longer the decisive ranger or gallant knight come to rescue the ladies. He waited at the door, hat in hand, and combed his fingers through his dark hair.

"You can wash up right here." Martha pulled a clean towel from a drawer, laid it on the counter and then moved out of the way. Far away. As far as she could go to the other side of the table to fill each cup with coffee and catch her breath. She set the pot on the table and took her seat as Haskell joined them with an unreadable expression.

Had he misspoken outside by the wagon? Did he regret hastily confessed emotions?

Keenly aware of him and feeling still the strength of his arms, his lips on her fingers and his breath on her face, she steadied herself as she raised her hand to his. Her father's strong grip encased her other hand, and his deep voice carried them all before the Lord.

"Thank You, Father, for bringing these three home safely. Thank You for Haskell's protection and help with the wagon, and for Whit's generosity. And thank You for Your grace and this food. Amen."

Mama must have told him about the snake. Martha prayed she hadn't mentioned Livvy's bold observations.

Her mother ladled soup into the men's bowls and Martha sliced the first pie and set a piece on each person's plate. The informality of their family meal relaxed her. An old Sunday school lesson came to mind of Jesus knocking at a door, asking to come in. As Livvy had that very day in her own home.

Martha regretted her immaturity and noted gratefully that everyone was intent on their meal and not her emotional fluctuations.

"So I hear you are a dead shot." Her father lifted his spoon to his mouth and his eyes to Haskell who, in turn, gave Martha a quick look. Gripping her coffee cup, she raised it to her lips and hid behind it.

"On occasion." Haskell spooned a mouthful.

"This one for sure, thank the Lord," her mother put in. "He fired once and that was that. I can't imagine what Martha and I would have done had we been alone."

Martha focused on the coffeepot. One shot had killed Joseph.

Coffee splashed onto her plate. She eased the cup to the table and prepared to excuse herself when her father's touch stopped her.

He leaned close, his voice a near whisper. "It's all right, Marti. You can do this. You can face it."

He held her with his dark eyes as well as his gentle hand. He was right. She could not keep running every time a gun was mentioned. She'd be running her entire life. She clasped her hands in her lap. Lord help her.

"Caleb, did I mention that Mr. Jacobs also rescued my apple butter jars unscathed from their trip over the gulley's edge?"

Thank you, Mama. Martha puffed out a tight breath and picked up her fork.

"That is a rescue, indeed." Her father raised a brow. "If you didn't get a chance to sample it, then you'll want to attend our fall basket social next Sunday after church. Annie always donates her last jars of the season to the fund-raiser. We'd love to have you."

It was bad enough that this family welcomed Haskell into their home on such equal standing. It was bad enough that Martha had not rebuffed him for his earlier empty-headed ramblings and sat within arm's reach. But now they had invited him to a social event. He, a gunman, a blatant reminder of what a bullet could do, and a man set on bringing in the one-time object of their daughter's affection.

That must be it.

Disappointment soured the sweet vinegar pie on the first bite. The custard melted in his mouth and slid down to land on the Huttons' ulterior motives.

With Tad Overton out of the picture, they could stop worrying about Martha and see that she was married off to a more respectable man. A younger, more stable person, like a banker or a merchant. Maybe that telegraph operator at the depot or a young farmer from their church.

As far as they were concerned, Haskell was just a hired gun with a badge, and they were paying him off with kindness. He choked on the pie.

All three Huttons looked at him.

"Did I add too much vinegar?" Concern edged Mrs. Hutton's voice.

"No." He set his fork down and coughed into his napkin. "No, pardon me. It's very good. It just went down the wrong pipe."

Martha's mouth tipped in an appealing way. Reaching for his coffee, he cut a glance at her mother, a physical prophecy of Martha's future. He stole a look at the pastor who, by all outward appearances, was a man at peace with God, himself and the world.

The evidence at the table said they were honest people with open hearts. So why did he suddenly mistrust them?

Angry for letting his emotions get the better of him, he excused himself a short time later, led Cache to the livery across the street and took a circuitous route back to the St. Cloud.

By the next Sunday, he was no closer to finding Tad Overton and more agitated than he could ever remember being. Concentration fled like a startled rabbit and he found himself retracing his steps and coming up empty.

Goldpan Parker had no news. No more horses had tromped through his camp in the middle of the night. Nor had there been any more in Doc's barn as far as Haskell could tell from sneaking around in the dark. He had even dropped word at the livery that he was looking for anyone who had come into ownership of new horses. The truth hit a high, strained pitch when he pulled his coat over his badge and insinuated he might be looking for a new mount.

But he could take no chances. The smithy knew everyone in town and then some. Which meant the man could tip off a friend and have him gone before Haskell saw his dust.

He looked in the glass that hung above his washstand. What had happened to his cold objectivity? Rubbing the linen towel over his face and across his hair, he formulated a telegraph for the captain. Maybe Overton had moved on. He needed to do the same. The more distance he put between himself and Martha Hutton, the clearer his thinking would be.

Decision made.

Tossing the towel aside, he pulled on his clean shirt and tucked it into his trousers. If he hadn't given Pastor Hutton his word, he'd ride out now. Instead, he was headed to a Sunday morning service and something called a basket social.

He'd leave that part out of the telegram.

Haskell set out for the church house at the other end of town, passing a much larger, elegant brick building on the way. Well-dressed people streamed inside the broad doors and a bell tower chimed out the fact that he was late. Another personal trait gone by the wayside since landing in Cañon City—promptness. He was losing his grip.

"Discipline." His father's admonition rang in the bells' aftertones. "Hunger. Temper. Loneliness." *Keep a tight rein on your desires. They'll lead you by the nose if you let them.*

Two blocks later, singing penetrated his dark mood and he mounted the steps to the church. The pews were filled, and several men stood at the back, hats in hand. Martha should be toward the front, if not in the very first pew.

Out of sight, out of mind.

Right.

She was as much out of his mind as she'd been out of his arms when he pulled her from Cache's back. Had he read more into her invitation to supper that night than she'd intended? Had his heart taken the bit in its teeth and run off with his common sense?

Songbooks closed like buckshot spitting across the sanctuary.

It didn't matter. He'd never pass the Huttons' muster for their daughter, even if she was of age.

"Please be seated." Pastor Hutton looked him in the eye and tipped his head in acknowledgment. A small red-haired woman delayed seating herself and glanced over her shoulder. Her shy smile pinned him to the wall as certain as a sharpshooter's trigger finger.

The man to his right snorted and slapped his hat against his leg. Haskell didn't recall meeting him, but something about him felt familiar. His slight frame, an impatient air bordering on disrespect. Haskell ran his hand through his hair and cut him a sideways glance. A smirk curled the younger's man's lip. Had he thought Martha smiled at *him?*

Maybe she had. The idea sobered Haskell and he pushed his shoulders back, straightened his stance.

"What is faith?" Hutton's voice reached all the way to the back of the cramped room, louder than Haskell had heard him before.

"Some say it's trust. Others say it's hogwash."

Several parishioners *tsked* and others snickered at the remark. In the few sermons Haskell had heard, the preacher hadn't used such common language. Maybe he'd been missing out all these years.

"Doesn't matter what some folks say. It matters what God says. And he's told us in the letter to the Romans that faith is the essence of what we hope for and evidence of what we can't see."

Haskell's attention rose at the word *evidence.*

"Faith is knowing. It's banking on what God tells us. It's proof of the invisible—like Him. We don't see God Himself, but we can see His handiwork around us and His love in our families and neighbors. We *know* He's with us."

Haskell understood evidence. But he also followed his gut at times without any real proof. Usually, he was right.

The young man snorted again. Haskell looked straight at him and conceit looked back. Haskell's hands began to sweat.

Chapter 13

He came.

But so had Tad. Martha would recognize those roguish good looks anywhere, though he'd aged considerably. But hadn't everyone?

And Haskell stood right next to him. Hopefully he wouldn't cause a scene during the sermon, throw Tad down and drag him away in shackles.

Martha twisted a wad of skirt into a wrinkled knot and then smoothed it out. She toed her basket from under her seat for another quick look at the wide blue ribbon encircling the wicker. A flamboyant bow blossomed on top, the same color as Haskell's eyes. She'd paid extra for that ribbon at the mercantile—against her grandmother's attempts to give it to her free of charge.

Her pulse kicked up. Would he notice? Did men see such things? Likely not. But he'd be sure to notice the fragrant fried chicken and fresh biscuits she could smell from where she sat.

Years ago she'd have stood on her head to get Tad's attention to buy her basket. Now he seemed like a mere boy standing at the back of the church next to Haskell. A boy much too sure of himself, if she read his expression correctly. She'd seen that look in her pupils' eyes, particularly young ruffians who thought they had pulled a prank she didn't know about.

Tad had not called on her since her return, nor had Martha seen him in town when she walked to the library or the mercantile. What was he up to these days? Could he really be stealing horses?

She pushed the basket beneath the pew and tried to concentrate on her father's sermon. Her childhood training to recite three points from the message had stayed with her all these years. She had even practiced it with Joseph—whose image fled her best efforts to bring him into focus. She strained to capture his features in her mind's eye and recall one of his many sermon topics.

"Faith is the substance of what we hope for." She blinked back to the present and her father standing behind the pulpit, obviously invigorated by the words he spoke.

All right, Lord. I get it. First Livvy, now Papa. God was indeed trying to get her attention.

But she'd always had faith. She grew up believing, knowing. Wasn't that enough?

"Let us pray."

Ashamed that she had missed so much of her father's message, she bowed her head and absorbed his benediction.

Afterward, all the women gathered at the front of the church, as was the custom for the fall basket social, and placed their ornately decorated baskets along the platform's edge. Martha glanced back at Haskell who stood oblivious to what was going on. She wanted *him* to bid on her basket. Not Tad or any other man, and not some old codger out to get a good meal, Lord forgive her.

"All right, ladies, please be seated toward the back of the room," her father said. "Gentlemen, step forward and we'll get under way. My stomach's empty as a new post hole, Mr. Russell, so kindly start the bidding."

Howard Russell, a rotund man with a bushy red mustache, stepped to the platform and shook her father's hand. An auctioneer who prided himself on the speed with which he could singsong people out of their money, he puffed out his already protruding chest and thumbed his suspenders. Her father lifted the first basket, and the bidding began.

Martha's agitation drove her from her seat. Who cared if she was being unseemly? She forced her feet into a dignified pace and strolled toward the back until she caught Haskell's eye. He leaned against the wall with no apparent intention of participating. Tad had disappeared.

She stopped next to Haskell and cleared her throat. When he made no comment, she glanced up at him. His jaw worked like a horse straining at the bit, his tension palpable. What had gotten into the man?

"Blue is my favorite color."

He looked down at her, arms folded across his chest, his black hat gripped in one hand.

Did she have to sketch it out for him? "I thought you might want to know."

"Oh." He pushed away from the wall and stood evenly on both feet. "All right."

He was obviously distracted. Maybe he'd figured out who had been standing right next to him. But wouldn't he have disappeared with his quarry if he'd known?

Tad's voice suddenly cut through the room. "Four bits."

Her basket dangled in her father's fingers, a not-so-happy expression on his face.

"Four bits, I have four bits," Mr. Russell sang. "Do I hear six bits a dollar?"

"Haskell."

He looked at her and realization dawned. "Six bits," he bellowed.

Several men turned to see who had bid and before they could turn back around, Tad barked, "One dollar."

Oh my. Martha's throat tightened. She may be dining with Tad Overton at one of the picnic tables scattered across her parents' front lawn. *Please, Lord. Please.*

"Two."

Haskell's booming bid made her jump. He threw a challenging glare toward the location of Tad's voice.

"Three!"

A murmur rippled through the congregants as they turned to gawk, and now everyone in the room saw her standing next to the tall stranger.

Why couldn't she have stayed in her seat with her mother?

Her mother. She searched for the woman and realized she was in the yard spreading tablecloths and setting up a lemonade stand on the porch. Martha should go help, but she couldn't pull herself away from the bidding war.

"Four."

She flinched. Haskell was willing to pay four dollars for her basket? Surely that would bring an end to this public display and they could enjoy her chicken in the quiet shade of her parents' giant elm tree.

Tad stood and held a shiny gold coin above his head. "I'll give the church a double eagle for that pretty little basket with the blue ribbon."

The room went deathly quiet. Martha's heart stopped, and Haskell tensed beside her. His left hand curled into a fist.

"It's all right," she whispered, hoping he could hear her. She touched his arm and it was hardened steel beneath her fingers. *Oh Lord, help us all.* The men mustn't come to blows right there in her father's church.

Haskell took a step forward and she dug her nails into his arm, forcing his attention to her. "It's all right. I don't mind. I mean—thank you."

The tension in his arm eased but his eyes burned with a hot, blue flame.

Mr. Russell slapped the pulpit as if prompted by the

Spirit. "Sold! For twenty dollars to the young man on my left. Come claim your prize, sir."

Martha shuddered at the insinuation. Her father's expression dared Tad to pry the basket from his hands. Tad's lips curled in what Martha had once considered a sly and secretive smile, but now it made her skin crawl. She released Haskell's arm and straightened her shoulders. How had Tad known?

"Mama's basket has a yellow ribbon and a yellow checkered cloth draped over the top." She couldn't be any clearer. If Haskell missed her cue, there was no helping him.

Martha waited by the door as Tad dropped the gold piece into Mr. Russell's hand and took the basket from her father—her kind and loving father, whom she'd never known to stare daggers at anyone, until now.

If Tad didn't read the warning, he was a fool.

Haskell's jaw ached and his fingers were numb. He'd squeezed the blood clean out of them. The silhouetted figure from Doc Mason's barn two weeks ago had outbid Haskell for Martha's basket. At great cost he reined in his temper.

He watched the thin man through slitted eyes. No wonder the palms of his hands were sweating. He'd been standing right next to the sidewinder through the whole sermon.

Tad sauntered to the back of the room, stopped and saluted Haskell with a finger to his forehead. Then he placed his hand intimately against Martha's elbow and directed her out the door.

Haskell nearly lunged for him over the possessive gesture. If Overton touched her in any other way...

Sudden laughter tore his attention from the door to Pastor Hutton holding a basket with a yellow ribbon. The impulse took him before he could reason it out.

"Ten dollars."

A collective gasp and the room stilled again.

The auctioneer twitched his mustache. "Well, the Hutton women have certainly drawn some serious bids today. Sold!" He slapped the pulpit and everyone applauded.

Haskell's steps bounced off the crowded pews as he strode forward and solemnly claimed his dinner. Pastor Hutton gripped his right hand and transferred the basket with the other. "Thank you for trying. I appreciate it."

"Three more baskets are all we've got left," Russell warned. "A few of you are going hungry today unless you can bribe someone into sharing."

Mrs. Hutton did not come forward. Haskell scanned the room and then recalled the pastor's mention of the parsonage yard. Maybe she was already there.

He trotted down the front steps and around the side of the church. Several tables were scattered across the clover lawn and couples and families were already seated, enjoying their meal. Martha's mother served lemonade from the near end of the porch, and another table stood empty at the opposite side. The perfect vantage point.

Overton and Martha sat beneath a large shade tree with Martha's back to the yard and Tad facing the group. He smirked as Haskell entered the front gate and walked toward the house.

Haskell ground his teeth, refusing to take the bait Overton dangled in his arrogant eyes. He could break the man like a matchstick and wanted to. But that would not serve the purpose of his assignment. Nor would it endear Martha Hutton to him. He may be just a hired gun as far as her parents were concerned, but he still cared for their daughter.

More than he should.

As his boot steps sounded on the porch, Mrs. Hutton looked up from her ladling. "Oh, Mr. Jacobs. How kind of you to bid on my basket. I hope you don't mind starting without me. Just have a seat at the table there, and I'll bring you a glass of lemonade."

He gave the cheerful woman a curt nod and attempted a smile.

Setting the basket on the table, Haskell seated himself at an angle so he could keep an eye on Overton. From the cover of his hat brim, he watched the scoundrel flash a brazen smile and lean low across the table, mouthing something only Martha could hear.

She moved discreetly backward every time Overton leaned toward her. Haskell grunted. If he weren't so drawn to her himself, the situation would be comical. Like a seesaw, the two of them leaned back and forth across the table. The signal was clear.

Mrs. Hutton brought the promised lemonade. "Please don't wait on my account, Mr. Jacobs. The chicken is cold already, but there is a jar of my apple butter tucked inside for the biscuits."

"Thank you, ma'am." He lifted his hat and quickly replaced it. "I'm sure everything will be as good as it smells."

She left him with a warm smile and a hand on his shoulder as she turned away. Evidence of—what?

He pulled the bow and the ribbon fell. Assuming the checkered cloth was a napkin, he set it aside and investigated the contents. A small jar nested in one corner and he set it on the table with two knives and forks. Two small plates of fried chicken followed, with another cloth holding several biscuits like those he'd had at the mercantile. He picked up one.

The memory raised his eyes to the pair seated under the tree and his gut twisted. Overton had moved to Martha's side of the table, straddling her bench.

The seesawing began again.

Martha scooted to her right. Overton followed. Haskell crushed the biscuit.

He glanced to see if Mrs. Hutton saw him destroying her food without eating it, but she was chatting with another woman and two small children holding their cups out expectantly.

He dusted the crumbs from his hands and reached for another biscuit just as Overton reached for Martha. Haskell's chair tipped back and he was off the porch by the time she had pushed the polecat away.

A sudden hush draped the yard and Haskell stopped inches from Overton, drilling him with a hard look as he spoke to Martha. "Miss Hutton, is everything all right?"

Overton's jaw clenched and his face reddened. He threw Haskell a dismissive wave. "Yeah. Everything's right as rain."

Haskell fisted his left hand, raised the other waist-level and held the edge of his coat. "I was speaking to the lady."

Overton swung his inside leg over the bench and rose to the challenge. A full head shorter, he was forced to look up. Anger brimmed in his eyes, and his hands opened and closed.

An easy read that could go one of two ways.

Instead of throwing a punch, Overton stepped back and stretched his lips in a cold smile. "Good to see you again, Marti. Maybe next time we can dine without interruption." He picked up his hat and leaned close to her ear. "And by the way, you and your dinner were worth every dollar."

He strode across the lawn, out the front gate and into the side street without looking back.

Picnickers resumed their pleasant conversations. Haskell breathed again.

Martha gathered her basket and stood. He offered his hand as she stepped over the bench and she took it and raised her eyes to his. "Thank you."

He placed his other hand atop hers. "Did he hurt you in any way?"

Her lips quivered in a slow, sad smile. "No, he did not hurt me. He simply opened my eyes to things I hadn't seen years ago. Perhaps I didn't want to then." She withdrew her hand and looked around at the others enjoying their Sunday afternoon.

"Would you join me on the porch? Your mother and I haven't eaten yet. She's been busy serving lemonade and I, well, I…"

"Yes, thank you." She held the basket with one hand and gathered her skirt with the other as they walked to the front steps. Her father was making the rounds of the tables crowding his front yard, thanking people for donating to the church's support for the coming winter.

And keeping one eye on his daughter and Haskell.

Chapter 14

Martha's heart raced and every inch of her skin tingled. She looked eastward for gathering storm clouds, but the only storm brewing did so in her jumbled thoughts. Haskell had rescued her *again*—this time from public humiliation, for she was about to shove Tad backward off the bench. Either that or stab him with her fork.

In a way, she pitied the boy who was stunted somehow, trapped in the same spot he was in when she'd left. He had aged, but he had not grown.

Martha took the stairs with Haskell close behind. Perspiration glimmered on her mother's forehead as she served a never-ending line of lemonade seekers. When Haskell joined her on the porch, Martha handed him her basket.

"Please take this and insist that Mama eat something. I'm going to take her place serving. She should also put her foot up, but—" Embarrassed, she glanced sideways at Haskell who looked like he'd been asked to attend a quilting bee.

"Never mind. Just make her eat something."

She stepped behind the serving table and took the ladle from her mother's hand. "Thank you, Mama. It's my turn. Haskell is waiting for you. Make sure he has some of your fine chicken and potato salad *before* he finishes off your apple butter."

Her mother dabbed her forehead with her apron hem

and gave Martha's shoulder a squeeze. "Perfect timing, dear. Perfect."

Martha's timing was not all that was perfect. She accepted a cup from a freckle-faced little boy and peeked at the tall, dark-haired man seating her mother at the table. She was developing a new definition of *perfect*.

She tipped the crock and ladled out enough to give the little boy a swallow. "That's it. You got the very last drop of lemonade."

He grinned his thanks and bounded down the stairs. Martha's father dodged quickly enough to avoid a collision with the freckle-faced lad, and then joined his wife and Haskell on the porch. Martha wiped her hands on a towel by the crock and did the same.

Taking her seat with a sigh, she relaxed for the first time that day. Relief washed over her like the afternoon sunshine, clarifying and defining more than the tables and people scattered across the yard. Martha was beginning to see herself in a different light, one that illuminated possibilities here in Cañon City, possibilities with a certain Colorado Ranger. If he chose to stay.

She pulled her basket closer and saw a pile of biscuit crumbs in the center of the table, brushed into a neat little pyramid. She cocked a brow at Haskell, who was busy working over a chicken leg, but her mother caught her question.

"That one didn't make it," she said with a laugh.

"Best social event of the year so far, Pastor." Foster Blanchard stood among her mother's peonies that fronted the porch, no doubt breaking off several stems. "I think your missus and daughter raised more for the coal-bin fund than the last two years put together."

Blanchard laughed at his cleverness, but as the church treasurer, he was probably right. Martha bent her head to a napkin hoping to avoid the need to comment.

"Don't forget," Blanchard continued. "We've got a bumper crop o' apples this year and I hate to see 'em go to waste. Come out and pick whatever you can haul off." He gave Martha's mother serious regard. "Best there is for that apple butter of yours, Mrs. Hutton. Right good."

"Thank you, Mr. Blanchard," her mother said. "We do appreciate it."

As the man blazed a path out of the peonies, she whispered, "He says that every year. I think he takes great pride in that apple butter."

"As do I," Martha's father said, squeezing his wife's hand.

"But I can't pick apples this year."

Martha felt the penetrating gaze, and a sense of foreboding shadowed the otherwise pleasant setting. Reluctantly she looked up from her napkin to see that she was right. Her mother spoke volumes in molasses-colored tones.

"You know I can't go hobbling around out in that man's orchard. Not with my ankle in the shape it's in." She blushed the slightest bit and lowered her eyes. "Pardon me, Mr. Jacobs, for speaking so personally."

Haskell coughed, caught unawares by the apology. "No pardon necessary, ma'am."

Martha scripted out the next comment before it hit the air.

"And your father can't go either, can you dear?" She gave him a look that only a husband could interpret, which he did quite skillfully.

"No, I'm sorry, but I can't." He reached for the last biscuit. "Too much to do around here in the next several days. And I need to get the church ready for winter." He spooned a large helping of apple butter onto his biscuit. "I guess that leaves you, Marti. If you can find someone to go with you, that is. I'd rather you didn't drive out to Blanchard's by yourself. Maybe one of the ladies from the library would like to pick apples. Or a student working the dig up at Finch's quarry."

Haskell seemed oblivious to their machinations. Not Martha. She'd ridden home on the train and she was about to be railroaded again with Haskell Jacobs, straight for Blanchard's apple orchard. Why must her parents interfere so blatantly?

She dropped her hands to her lap and opened her mouth to speak, but Haskell picked up the trail.

"Might I accompany your daughter to the orchard?" He looked her father in the eye as if she were not sitting at the table with them. As if she were twelve and he needed permission to go with her. Of all the—

"A wonderful idea, Mr. Jacobs." Her mother smiled demurely, effectively masking the manipulative nature that lurked just below a glowing surface.

Haskell turned to Martha as she fumed. "What day would you like to go?"

His question demanded a clear answer and his laughter-laced eyes banished her anger. A day with Haskell? She should be so fortunate. He was indeed stealing her heart. But could she trust him?

Doubt slipped a cold hand around her neck and reminded her that she knew very little about the man. But she knew quite a bit more about Tad Overton and she'd take Haskell's company over Tad's any day.

"Wednesday." That day required them to return in time for the midweek service and thus ensured they'd be home before dark. And it left two days open for a trip to the fossil quarry.

"Wednesday it is."

"I shall pack a lunch for you," her mother said. "It's the least I can do."

Martha rolled her eyes and wondered if Haskell had any idea he'd been set up.

* * *

Monday morning's nine-mile ride to the fossil site in Mr. Winton's cab proved dustier and rougher than Martha remembered from her youth. Then again, at her age with a still-sensitive shoulder, she was not the young woman she'd been at seventeen.

Enthusiasm seemed to have waned over the dig, as her mother had suspected, for few people joined the excursion. Golden cottonwoods and aspen paraded along the creek bed that marked the road into the red canyon, and bold blue sky reminded her that fall reigned in the wide Arkansas Valley.

At the wash that held the quarry, Mr. Winton was careful to hand her down from the cab and lead the way up the ravine to the site. With her sketchpad under her arm, she paused to tie on the bonnet her mother had insisted she take. The sun made a furnace of the hard-baked earth and yellow stone that formed the gully's walls. Not a green thing grew at the dig site other than stunted juniper trees that clung with gnarled fingerlike roots to barren rock.

From a distance, Mr. Finch looked much the same as she remembered, hunched over his work with a small pick and brush, pitifully shaded by his soiled farmer's hat. Hesitant to lose her footing on the loose shale, she held back as others ventured across the site to join in the careful digging and brushing. She situated herself on a large flat rock to sketch the scene before her, careful to mind the details.

The place had lost much of its appeal. It looked the same, but the intriguing mystery of what lay beneath the ancient streambed had been replaced by wonder at what stirred in her heart regarding a certain, very much alive, Colorado Ranger.

Not much in Haskell's Monday telegram to Captain Blain resembled the one he'd planned Sunday before church. Nor was it the only thing that had changed since then.

He slid the paper across the counter, followed by a coin. Outside the train station he lingered, watching people buy tickets and leave trunks on the platform. He'd hoped to be leaving by this time as well, with a prisoner cuffed to his arm and Cache tied in a boxcar. His original purpose in Cañon City had faded next to his growing affection for Martha Hutton and he needed to get back on track. Lack of discipline had him hobbled.

That accounted in part for nearly wadin' into Tad Overton in the parson's front yard. He'd let a beautiful woman distract him. The case might have been wrapped up, with the crook in custody, if he hadn't been drawn off course by the widow's charm.

He huffed, looked up the street and then crossed toward the café. Nothing about Martha Hutton said *widow* any longer. In two weeks' time she had shed her dark dresses, and her pale features had warmed. Just that morning he'd trailed her and a group of bone hunters to the bluffs in what the locals called Garden Park. Who spent all day in the sun digging for dead animals, regardless of how large the bones were?

Martha Hutton, for one. He stomped his boots outside the café door and entered to a full house. One small table sat empty in the far corner. The perfect spot to no one but him.

With his back to the wall and a clear view of the door, he ordered steak and eggs and coffee and was pleased to see that the meal also came with a pile of fried potatoes. He forked the eggs onto the steak and dug in.

He needed a plan. If Overton had sold off the stolen horses—demonstrated by the double eagle he'd brandished in church Sunday—how could Haskell prove the man was the culprit? He needed evidence.

He shoved down a curse unspoken, a recent tendency inspired by intrusive thoughts of Martha, her family and their God.

It wasn't that he didn't believe. Of course he believed. But God didn't get involved in his work and Haskell didn't invite him to. He stabbed the steak with his fork and cut off a chunk.

Whit Hutton had mentioned Texas Creek. It was worth a half-day's ride up the canyon to find out who had bought the horses, and it had to be tomorrow. Wednesday he was picking apples.

He shook his head at the yellow yolk bleeding across the meat. The Huttons were good. Very good. He chuckled, remembering Martha's discomfort at the table as they herded her toward a hired-gun chaperone.

"Something funny?"

The aproned waiter stood with a steaming coffeepot and a puzzled frown.

"No." Haskell wiped his mouth and then held his cup out. "Thanks."

The man considered him with suspicion, but Haskell did not explain anything to anybody he didn't work for. With a sniff and a shake of his head, the waiter moved off to another table

It wouldn't hurt to stop in and check with the sheriff again. He was aware of Haskell's assignment, and if he wasn't in cahoots with the thief, he might have heard something and be willing to exchange information.

He certainly wasn't out beating the bushes for the snake. Fact was, Haskell didn't know what the sheriff did, other than gouge the top of his desk with his spurs. A man didn't need spurs if he didn't ride—unless he just liked the sound of his own janglers.

And that was how Haskell found him when he walked into the sheriff's office after breakfast. Feet up on the desk, hat slouched over his face, fingers laced across his belly. Haskell slammed the door and watched the man scramble to keep from tipping backward.

"Morning, Sheriff." Making enemies wasn't Haskell's way, but this man wasn't smart enough to be his enemy.

"Jacobs." The sheriff coughed and sputtered and righted his hat. "Ya find your horse thief yet?"

"No, that's why I stopped in. Wondered if you'd heard anything."

The sheriff stood, hitched his britches and walked to the board where he displayed wanted posters. He mumbled the names to himself and then walked back to his desk chair, spurs a-janglin'. "Can't say that I have."

Or wouldn't say.

"Have you heard talk of any new horseflesh around? Anyone buy a few head lately with blistered brands? Like maybe up around Texas Creek?"

The sheriff cut his eyes sideways and pulled on the end of his mustache. "Nope. Not lately. 'Course we don't hear much from up the canyon without ridin' up there, seein' as how they ain't got no telegraph 'til Salida."

Haskell reset his hat and turned for the door. "Thanks anyway."

The desk chair creaked. "Say, Jacobs. You thinkin' of stayin' in these parts? Settlin' down, maybe?"

Haskell faced him. "Why do you ask?"

"Well, election's comin' up this fall. They'll be needin' a sheriff, seein' as how I'm goin' back to Missouri. Thought you might be interested in the position, you bein' a lawman yourself and all."

The man had more nervous twitches than an old woman on chewing tobacco. "That right?" Haskell folded his arms. "No takers around here?"

The sheriff snorted. "Can't get nobody. Ain't enough

goin' on around here to keep a man busy. Not worth the trouble."

That depended on the correct definition of *trouble*. Haskell reached for the door. "Thanks for the tip. I'll think about it."

He thought about it the rest of the day.

And all the next. He thought about it while he brushed and saddled Cache and rode to Texas Creek. He thought about how he could find that place he wanted and raise a few cows, maybe a couple of youngsters like Whit and Livvy's boys.

And build a house with a porch that faced the sunset.

He pressed a fist against an ache in his chest.

As he rounded the bend to the junction, a small park spread out from the river and the mountains leaned back against a clear sky. A mighty hand had cut this land and forested these slopes. A hand Haskell could use right now.

He cleared his throat, rubbed his jaw. "Lord."

Cache's ear twitched back at the sound.

"I know we haven't spoken much lately, but I'd be obliged if You'd turn me in the right direction where Overton is concerned."

The horse shook his head and jerked on the reins.

"And help me win Martha's hand."

Cache nickered.

Fool horse was laughing at him. "Amen."

Yellow cottonwood trees flared along the river, their gold leaves quivering like paper coins against a blue sky. Autumn's sharp edge cut the fine air, and a lungful invigorated Haskell as he climbed off his horse at the Texas Creek General Store.

A man had ridden through the week before with a string of ponies, the storekeep told him. "Wouldn't have minded havin' the little mare for myself," he said as he stacked canned peaches on a shelf behind the counter. "Green broke, fresh branded." He faced Haskell with the air of a busy proprietor. "But I don't got time to be breakin' no horses."

"What did this man look like?"

"Younger than you. Thin, dark hair. When he came back through he didn't have the horses."

"Any idea who he sold them to?"

"Rancher, I expect. But wouldn't know which one. I'll ask around, though. Send word if I hear."

Haskell drew a pencil and paper out of his coat, wrote his name and handed it to the man.

The storekeep read it. "Tillman," he said, and glanced up.

"I'm at the St. Cloud. They'll take a message."

On the way down the mountain, Haskell studied on how he'd explain having two last names if he ran for sheriff.

If Martha Hutton would have him.

Chapter 15

In the last two weeks, Martha had joined the Women's Reading Club, helped at the mercantile and rode up to the Finch quarry north of town. Between helping her mother and keeping up with her new activities, she'd found herself thinking less and less about Joseph.

She pulled the hairbrush through loose tangles, closed her eyes and tried to picture him as he brushed her hair in the evenings. Though she loved him still, his features more often blurred and melted into a murky memory. She plaited the long strands and coiled the braid at the base of her neck to keep it from snagging on tree branches or falling across her face. A full day's work awaited her. A full day with Haskell Jacobs.

A shiver ran up her back and her gaze fell on the matching brush set on her dressing table. Blue forget-me-nots trailed around pink and yellow roses on the porcelain backing. Was she forgetting? Was she being unfaithful to consider another man?

"Martha?"

Mama might push into her affairs, but she never burst through her closed door.

"Come in, I'm up."

Aproned and wide awake from preparing breakfast, her mother sat on the edge of the bed and smoothed invisible wrinkles in the colorful quilt. "I remember when we made this and how often I had to soak out bloodstains from your pricked fingers."

Martha chuckled and sat down to pull on her boots. "It took me a while to get the feel for the thimble, didn't it?"

Her mother had not come up before breakfast lately, so something itched to get out beyond Papa's hearing. Martha pushed a stockinged foot into one boot and began pulling the laces.

"I'm sorry I can't go with you today."

Martha paused, then continued tightening the laces. She'd never known her mother to be untruthful, but the woman was stretching the facts as tight as Martha stretched the black strings in her fingers.

"Please be careful."

Tempted to jump into a tirade about her parents manipulating the entire situation, Martha sat up and regarded her mother. Two lines creased between the woman's brows and unruly gray wisps flared from her hairline.

"If you are truly worried about me in Haskell's company, why did you and Papa work so hard at getting him to take me to Blanchard's orchard today?"

Her mother spread reddened fingers on her lap and studied them against her apron. "What I meant to say is, be careful with your heart." She glanced at Martha's small fossil collection. "Don't keep it on a shelf as a monument to the past. Be open to what the Lord might have in store for you."

All the breath left Martha's chest. This was not the usual mother-daughter talk she had suffered through during her schoolgirl years, pining over Tad Overton.

Her mother folded her hands and raised her chin. Martha tensed.

"God has given us a great capacity to love, but the choice is ours. I love both you and Whit more than I can explain. Differently, yet the same. One of you is not loved more than the other. And now Livvy and the boys have my love as well."

Martha tied off the first boot and reached for the second. "But you've had only one *husband*. Could there ever have been anyone else?"

"That's a hard question, I know. And I've not been faced with that loss, as you have." Her voice softened and yearning filled her eyes. "You will always love Joseph, but you have enough love for Haskell as well. And loving him in Joseph's absence from this earth does not mean you are betraying Joseph."

Martha tugged on the laces as her heartstrings tightened in her chest. Her doubts did not suddenly fly out the window, but they tested their wings.

She tied off the second boot, then stood and held out her hands. "Thank you, Mama. I think the Lord must have sent you up this morning."

A quick embrace and she stepped back to press one more question. "But why Haskell? You don't know him any better than I do."

Her mother pushed at her hair combs, then turned to smooth the bed where they had been sitting. Straightening, she looked Martha in the eye—a mirrored look that sent chills up Martha's arms.

"I have never seen you more yourself than when you are in his presence." With that she turned and left Martha standing by the bed, feeling less a daughter and more a woman than she ever had before.

By the time they finished washing the breakfast dishes, the clop of horse's hooves echoed off the barn. Towel in hand, Martha looked through the door glass. Haskell dismounted at the corral and looped his horse's reins over the rail. Papa was readying the wagon and Haskell led Dolly from the barn, already harnessed, and backed her between the shafts. The men worked in tandem, as if each read the other's thoughts. Like Martha and her mother.

She dried her hands and patted her hair.

"Take my new hat." Her mother lifted the broad-brimmed straw from the hooks by the door. "You don't want to look like a baked apple after spending all day in the sun."

"Thank you. I really need to get one of my own, but I don't think of it when I'm at the mercantile." She tried it on and hurried to the mirror in the front hall. With a nervous giggle, she tied the ribbons beneath her chin. All she needed was a daisy in the hatband.

The back door opened and Martha's heart stopped. Why did such a divided pathway seem to stretch before her? Only one road led to Blanchard's apple orchard east of town, but she sensed she'd be choosing between two that day.

Lord, help me choose well.

When she entered the kitchen, Haskell's face warmed with—what? Was he laughing at her foolish hat, spreading nearly over her shoulders?

"You're ready." A pleased expression pulled at his mouth and his eyes darkened. He curled the edge of his hat brim, held loosely in one hand.

Her mother handed her the picnic basket and gave her a peck on the cheek. "Don't be late for services."

"We won't."

Haskell gave his characteristic nod and stepped aside for Martha to exit.

A crisp fall morning greeted her. Stacked bushel baskets filled half the wagon bed and she set the picnic lunch beneath the bench seat and shoved it to the center. A handy distance for reaching from the ground, plus a safe divider.

The memory of Tad's inappropriate advances at the social on Sunday shuddered through her.

"Martha." Her mother stood on the back porch holding a quilt and Martha's light wrap.

"I'll take them," Haskell said, reaching for the bundle.

He laid the quilt and Martha's cloak in the nearest bushel basket, then offered his hand. Warm and strong, it gripped hers as she climbed up, and he steadied her elbow with the other.

Safe. He made her feel safe. Protected.

The wagon creaked and swayed slightly when he pulled himself in and settled beside her, kicking the picnic basket with his foot. He looked down and a slight twitch tugged at his mouth. A warm blush swept her cheeks and she turned her head, grateful for the wide brim.

He gathered the reins, flicked the mare's rump and they set off at a lazy pace down the lane, east onto Main Street and into the open country that stretched between town and the Blanchards' farm. It would take at least a half hour before they reached the sheltered valley where apple orchards quilted the fertile landscape.

The sun warmed her hands and her body, and cloudless skies promised a fine clear day. As they jostled along, Martha looked over her shoulder and counted the bushel baskets. They assured several hours of hard, hot work in the kitchen. *Love's labor,* her mother called apple harvest, with its cooking and canning and drying and baking.

The hat prevented any sideways glances at her companion, but on pretense of scanning the countryside, she turned her head enough to study his profile. Strong. Kind. No tension in his jaw. No coat, just his vest but without the star. He seemed genuinely relaxed, and a slow smile lifted his mouth. Quickly, she looked ahead.

A soft laugh rumbled deep beside her. She straightened her back and stared at Dolly's bobbing head.

"This road is smoother than the one to your brother's ranch, wouldn't you say?"

She felt his gaze and chanced a quick glance. The coil that was her stomach loosened. "Much. Even if we came across a sunning rattlesnake, we wouldn't risk turning over."

Startled by her unwitting mention of the snake, she looked at his hip. As always, his gun lay easy there. She hadn't spotted it earlier. It was such a part of him that she no longer noticed it at all.

Feeling bundled up tight, Martha untied the ribbon and set the hat aside.

"Much better." He washed her hair and face with a look that rippled clear through her.

Her cheeks warmed again, but replacing the hat would send the wrong message. "I'll need the hat later, when the sun is higher and relentless. Right now it feels good on my face."

"It *looks* good on your face."

Leave it to Haskell to speak his mind so easily. This outing might turn out to be more than she expected. She needed to keep the conversation on safe ground. "Have you picked apples before?"

He laughed aloud. Free of mockery, the sound encased them, drawing them together in a shared and secret moment. Something feathery brushed against her heart.

Haskell slapped the reins on the lagging mare. At this point in his life, he figured he'd done most everything that qualified as new and adventurous. Apple picking wasn't one of those things, but he fully counted on it to top the list.

"No, this is my first venture to an apple orchard, but I'm sure it will be worth the day's work for the pies and apple butter I've sampled at your table." And the uninterrupted time spent with a woman whose cheeks bore the same tender glow as the smooth, firm fruit.

They topped a rise and orchards spread before them in

blocky green patches, some edged with a tarnished warning that the season was changing. Farmhouses and barns peeked out of scattered clearings, and dogs barked in the distance. Martha clapped her hands.

"I love this part—the surprise of seeing the valley so green and full and awaiting harvest." She took a deep breath. "Can you smell it? The rich, sweet nectar?"

He inhaled and drew in only dust from the mare's steady hoofbeats. "Not exactly." He coughed.

Martha laughed and leaned toward him. That picnic basket would *not* be between them on the ride back to town.

"I'm sure it's my imagination. Or anticipation. But this is the only fun part of picking apples. Everything else is a lot of hard work."

"But it has great rewards." He glanced at her sideways.

"As you said, you've never picked apples. Wait until you're up a tree with the fruit just out of reach and you risking your neck if you take another step."

He groaned at the irony. She looked at him full-on. "Is something wrong?"

"No." He shook his head and chuckled. "You just have a way with words."

"Well, I was a teacher, you know."

"No, I didn't." But he should have. "Why aren't you teaching now, here in Cañon City?"

She folded her hands and straightened her back. "I wanted to do something different, at least for a while. So I joined the Women's Reading Club and I went on an excursion to the fossil dig and I hope to teach drawing to anyone interested in landscapes."

At least he knew some of those things. "Sounds like you have plenty to do without adding teaching to your list."

She smiled up at him and his backbone turned to applesauce. She had more power over his nerves than any gun slick he'd ever faced.

"Maybe after Christmas. Mama and I will be busy enough canning and preserving for the next few weeks. November and December are full of preparation for the holidays. In January it will be too cold to go up to the quarry. Maybe the schools can use an extra teacher when classes start again."

"How did you become interested in dinosaur bones?"

She cupped her hands like a bowl on her lap and gazed into them. "Years ago the curio shop in town had fossils displayed that area ranchers had dug up on their land. It was like a miniature museum. Professors from eastern universities came to see the massive bones and they eventually set up digs in a heated race over who could find the best specimens. Wagon load after wagon load of gigantic bones were shipped to museums around the country. I was fascinated by the evidence of creatures that lived so long ago but no longer roamed this country. Or any country, for that matter."

The wagon's wheel hit a washout and at the sudden jolt, Martha gripped his leg. Catching herself, she quickly withdrew her hand and looked away. "Pardon me. I guess I'm jumpier than I thought."

If that infernal picnic basket wasn't wedged beneath the bench, he'd pull her closer.

"Don't worry. You won't hurt me."

She gasped at his presumption and shot him a wicked glare that quickly turned mischievous. "Wait until I've got you up an old apple tree, Mr. Jacobs."

Wait until I've got you in my arms. He rubbed a hand over his face, hoping to clear the fog. He hadn't even checked for anyone following. Where was his head?

He glanced behind them to an empty road. His best

opportunity was the top of the hill, but they were already down the far side and into the valley.

"Turn into the next farm on the left. That will be the Blanchards' place. He has ladders in his barn that we always use, so stop there first."

"Yes, ma'am." He flicked the mare into a trot and they turned down a tree-lined lane that rivaled groves he'd seen in the East. Driving into a different world, they were immediately swallowed by apple trees. A winelike perfume suffused the air. "I smell it now."

"Told you."

Her childlike anticipation infected him. Surrounded as they were by a lush orchard, it was easy to forget his job as a ranger. And he planned to do just that. At least for a day.

He pulled up at a neat red barn with green wagons parked nearby, and Blanchard himself ambled through the broad double doors in his dungarees, a pitchfork in hand. He swiped his head with a forearm but failed to hide his surprise at Haskell's presence.

"Mornin', Miss Hutton. I see you've come to get those apples." He took in the bushel baskets. "I expected your mama to be with you."

Haskell jumped to the ground and waited at the mare's head.

"She wanted to come, but her ankle still bothers her from a fall she took the other day." Martha gestured to Haskell. "Mr. Jacobs here kindly agreed to help. May we borrow one of your ladders?"

Apparently satisfied that Haskell hadn't kidnapped Martha and brought her out against her will, Blanchard grunted something and motioned for Haskell to follow him into the barn. A moment later Haskell shouldered a ladder and a long pole and laid them in the wagon bed.

"Thank you, sir," he told the farmer. "We'll bring them back before we leave."

He climbed in and picked up the reins. "Which way?"

Martha twisted in the seat and looked around. "I want the Gano variety. They ripen first and are good for nearly everything, but if I remember correctly, they're out a ways." She pointed to a narrow lane that led away from the barn. "Take that path."

They drove deeper into the orchard where most trees hung full with green apples just beginning to ripen. As they continued, the fruit darkened to a bright red. "Here," she said. "Pull up here and we can pick a few and see how they taste."

Before Haskell had a chance to loop the reins on the brake handle, Marti hopped to the ground, hiked her skirt and made a beeline for the nearest tree. The woman wasted no time once she saw what she wanted.

Would she ever want him?

By midday, he'd climbed enough trees to appreciate good footing. He'd poled branches, knocked apples to the ground and helped Martha scoop them into an apron she'd brought and dump them into the baskets.

As she took off toward the next tree, he raised both hands in surrender. "Enough!"

She whirled and rested her hands at her waist. "Are you surrendering? Is that it, Mr. *Ranger?*"

He'd soon be loco with that playful look and taunting voice. No child on a schoolyard had a chance with her, much less a man like him.

"Guilty as charged." He dropped his hands. "I'm starving."

Her eyes flashed and she stooped to pick up a fallen apple. One eyebrow cocked like a pistol, and she bounced the red orb playfully. "Why not have an apple?"

"I wouldn't do that if I were you."

Innocence washed over her features and she tilted her head. "Do what?"

He ducked and the apple hit him in the arm. "That."

Laughter bubbled into her eyes and out of her mouth and she grabbed her skirt in both hands and bolted away.

He was supposed to be chasing an outlaw, not a red-haired beauty flying through an apple orchard with her lace-up boots peeking beneath her skirts. Her laughter rolled behind her like the Sirens' song and he was helpless to go anywhere else but after her.

Out of breath, she stopped behind a tree and circled one way as he circled the other. He lunged, then switched back, catching her off guard. She screamed and turned, but too late. He caught her left arm and she jerked around into him, falling against his chest, laughing and gasping for breath.

Without thinking, he cupped her head in his hand and pressed his mouth against hers. Sweeter than any apple, the taste of her drowned all reason.

He lifted his head and pulled her closer, her chest heaving, her hands pressed against him but not resisting. Then she looped her arms around him and laid her head on his chest. And all of heaven and earth stood still in the circle of his arms.

Chapter 16

Martha's heart pounded against her ribs and Haskell's hammered in her ear. He held her as if she might fly away, and, at that moment, she did not doubt that her emotions had taken flight.

He played. Without hesitation, he'd chased her and laughed with her and kissed her senseless. She had yet to judge if he was merely toying with her.

If her parents' approval was any indication, Haskell Jacobs was an honorable man. The day would tell.

She pushed gently. His arms fell from around her, but his eyes imprisoned her in a blue gaze she had no desire to flee. Yet like a jealous child, doubt whispered in her ear, *He'll soon be leaving.* The truth of the words weighed on her spirit and she shook the dust from her skirts to shake the words from her mind. "We'd best be getting back to the wagon and our lunch."

She turned to lead the way and stopped short. In the chase, she'd lost all sense of direction. Even the mountains were hidden from view, surrounded as they were by row after row of apple trees. Fear sneaked in and pressed close to doubt.

"What is it?" Concern deepened Haskell's voice and he reached for her hand. He must have discerned what taunted her, for he smiled and bent her fingers in his elbow. "This way."

He watched the ground as they walked. Of course. He

was tracking their steps. Martha studied the path he took between the trees but saw no signs of anything other than grass and bird-pecked apples fallen from their branches. The sun bore straight down upon them. So much for her mother's garden hat.

And then she heard the mare nicker.

"Oh." Relief huffed out and she fingered her bodice. Haskell's hand tightened atop hers and she looked up.

Stopping, he turned to face her and took both her hands in his. "I told you once before that I will never hurt you. I meant that. Nor will I let anyone or anything—like being lost—hurt you."

Never. That was a long time. A word she'd cautioned her students not to bandy about. Did Haskell use it lightly or did he mean it?

Without taking his eyes from hers, he lifted one hand to his lips as he had before. Her breath fled at the gesture and she fought for stability. Which was more demanding—running through the orchard or yielding to his touch?

His stomach growled and Martha giggled, setting them both free from the moment. She withdrew her hand and hurried to the wagon for the picnic basket. He followed and retrieved the quilt.

Kneeling on the bright patchwork Haskell spread on the ground, Martha unpacked two small crocks of chicken potpie, molasses cookies and a jar of lemonade. She gave him a fork, a napkin and one of the pies, and set the cookies and lemonade between them. Two empty apple-butter jars served as glasses.

Martha poked through her pie crust, but Haskell waited. She looked at him, expecting some disappointing word about chicken. But he'd eaten it at the social on Sunday. Surely he wasn't put off by what her mother had packed.

Then she remembered and set her pie aside. "Would you like to offer thanks or shall I?"

He held out his hand and she took it. He linked his fingers through hers and bowed his head. "Thank You, Lord, for this day and this food and this company. Amen."

She kept her eyes shut tight, but the smile burst from within. Haskell had followed her father's lead on prayers that were brief and to the point. "Amen."

Mama had outdone herself. If Martha ate all of her serving, she'd not be able to finish filling the few bushels that remained empty in the wagon. Already she longed to lie back on the patchwork quilt and nap in the shade.

But a lady did not fall asleep in an orchard alone with a man other than her father or husband, regardless of how honorable that man might be. Goodness, as it was, Mr. Blanchard was sure to set the gossip fires burning over her traipsing into his orchards unescorted by a family member.

But she was no young, inexperienced girl. She glanced at Haskell, who had given in to the urge to stretch out and close his eyes. He'd linked his hands beneath his head and dark lashes rested on his tanned face. How tempted she was to lean down and return the kiss he'd given her. How easily she could lay her head on his broad chest and close her eyes to the beating of his heart.

Heat rushed up her neck and she reached for the lemonade. Such thoughts should be reserved for one's husband. And what made her think he'd ever consider a match between them? He knew little of her background and she knew less of his, and nothing of his intentions for that matter.

A kiss or two did not a proposal make.

What if he intended to leave after he caught the horse thief? As much as she had resisted believing that Tad was the culprit, she could see he fit the pattern. His sudden appearance with a twenty-dollar gold piece laid suspicion at his feet. He could have been stealing horses for years and

Martha wouldn't know any different. Maybe the Colorado Rangers had good reason to be on his heels.

She reached again for the lemonade jar and Haskell's eyes opened. He sat up and stretched his arms overhead, flexing his shoulders and hands.

"So when will you arrest Tad?"

Her question stilled his movements and his eyes narrowed. A ranger's mask slipped across his face, just as it had the first day she'd asked him what he was doing in Cañon City.

"Does it matter?"

Blunt, if nothing else. At least he spoke his mind. In that way, they were much the same, except propriety kept her from speaking her mind as far as he was concerned.

"I suppose not," she lied, careful to look anywhere but into his piercing gaze. "I just thought you'd take him back to Denver or wherever you take your prisoners and go home to…wherever home is."

He watched her for a long moment and she dreaded what he might say—leaving tomorrow, never returning, moving on to the next assignment. She sipped her lemonade.

"I'd like to settle down here."

Coughing like a sick cow, she sloshed the contents of her short jar onto her lap and the quilt. She covered her mouth with one hand and sopped up the spill with her apron.

"Would it be that bad to have me around?"

She flashed him an embarrassed look and saw that he was dead serious.

"No. You…you just surprised me. I expected…"

"What did you expect?"

She'd better close her mouth before she talked herself into a corner.

"I don't know what I expected."

"But you do know you're a terrible liar, don't you?"

The heat in her face rivaled the cookstove with a full

kettle of apples, and she regretted not grabbing her hat. Very well. If he wanted to play this kind of chase, she'd join him. She untied her wet apron and stuffed it into the picnic basket, then began packing their dishes and leftovers. He snatched the cookies before she got to them and shoved one in his mouth whole.

"I expected you to leave. To go on to your next assignment. I dare say Cañon City does not often draw infamous hoodlums to the river's banks, though we have had some trouble with vandals up at the quarry lately."

He crossed his legs Ute-fashion and bit into another cookie while watching her. She closed the basket and made to stand. He stopped her with a light touch.

His gaze brushed across her hair and cheek and neck, leaving as much heat in its wake as the summer sun at noon.

"The sheriff asked if I'd be interested in running for office. He's going back to Missouri after the election."

Haskell Jacobs had a knack for stealing her breath, either with his lips or with what those lips had to say. "What did you tell him?"

"I told him I'd think on it."

"Well." Profound for a schoolteacher. She could have said nearly anything, like "Please do" or "Would you?" or "You'd be a wonderful sheriff." The last phrase nearly slipped out but he stopped her short.

"What do *you* think?"

The verbal chopping block's rough surface scraped Haskell's neck and he swallowed hard. Never once had he asked someone other than his father what they thought he should do. But he wanted to know, needed to know this time. It meant the difference between riding out and coming back or just riding out.

He'd catch Tad Overton, that was certain. Either in the

act or through a witness. But what he did after that was up to Pastor and Mrs. Hutton's widowed daughter. If she'd have him, he'd stay. If not, he'd never look back.

Fear took a choke hold on his belly.

Mixed emotions warred across her features—the fear and doubt he'd seen when she thought they were lost, and another he hoped was yearning. One word, just one was enough.

She fumbled with her skirt and folded and unfolded her hands. Each gesture tightened the grip on his gut.

Finally, she took a breath and held it in, then met him eye to eye. "I'd like it very much if you decided to run for sheriff."

The grip broke with such force he felt gut-kicked. The air rushed out of him and he held up a hand and waited as breath seeped into his lungs. "There's only one problem."

She wadded her skirt in her fists and straightened her back as if bracing for a blow. He should have told her and her parents long ago.

"Different people in town know me by two different names."

She stared, her lips parted, her brows drawn. "What do you mean?"

"My name is Haskell Jacobs. But it is also Haskell Tillman Jacobs. Sometimes I go by Haskell Tillman—at the hotel, the café, the livery. With others, I use Haskell Jacobs."

A sigh escaped her perfect mouth and her shoulders relaxed. "I see." One hand fingered her bodice. "You frightened me. I thought you had deceived us."

"In a way I have. I should have told you and your family the whole truth. Then I wouldn't have to explain it when I ask for your hand."

Her fingers stilled and she regarded him with doubt.

He reached across the picnic basket for those fingers. "If you will have me."

She blinked, rolled her lips together and peered into the orchard behind him. Interlocking her small hand in his, she drew her eyes to his and favored him with a warm smile. "Yes, Haskell Tillman Jacobs. I will."

He laughed and pushed the basket aside. She came willingly into his arms, and he kissed the top of her head. To do more would lead him into dangerous territory, and he had given his word.

Could it really be this easy? Had God really answered his prayer?

She eased back and spread her skirt over her feet. "Did Whit tell you anything about my marriage?"

Uncertainty edged her voice. Guilt called for his confession, but he wanted to hear her version, get that glimpse into her heart. He resisted the urge to pull the pins from her hair and let the braid fall over her shoulder. "I'd like to hear it from you."

She tugged at a loose quilt thread. "I was Mrs. Joseph Stanton for two wonderful years. Joseph pastored a small church in St. Louis and I taught school. One afternoon early last fall, Joseph was in town on church business and left late to come home. Near dark."

She drew in a shaky breath and continued in a careful tone, as if unfolding an old and faded letter. "He stepped out to cross the street and a bullet from a drunkard's gun hit him in the back of the head." Her voice dipped. "We had no children."

Haskell ached to hold her, to kiss away the pain that etched her face, to shield her from the world's evil.

"Your gun put me off for quite some time, but I am grown-up enough to know that not all men who carry guns use them for ill purposes. It may take me a while to become accustomed to one so close, but I am willing to try."

A smile trembled on her lips and his heart twisted. He would die protecting her, if need be. But he preferred to live out his life as her husband.

"I'll not be able to set it aside if I am elected sheriff."

She closed her eyes. "I know. But it's who you are. I cannot ask you to be anyone other than who you are."

He pulled her to him and simply held her until the mare whinnied them back to the moment. Time had kept its steady pace and already the sun had slipped past its zenith. He stood and helped her to her feet, and they packed the basket and quilt in the wagon bed. She leaned over the back, surveying what they'd accomplished.

Only two bushel baskets remained empty. They could hurry to fill them or come back another day, but he might not get that chance. It was his fault they hadn't finished.

He lifted a bushel over the edge.

"It's all right, Haskell." She moved to the mare and stroked its shoulder. "We have plenty. We'll need to unload before dark anyway, and I'd rather enjoy the trip back than overwork Dolly trying to get her home too quickly with a full load."

A metallic click lifted the hair on Haskell's neck. The basket dropped and he slapped his holster.

"Ah-ah-ah." The voice closed in and a gun barrel pressed between his shoulder blades as a hand slipped his Colt from the leather. It landed among the trees with a dull thud. "Have a seat, Ranger Tillman."

Martha froze beside the mare, her face pale as death. "Tad."

"Why, darlin', I'm so glad you're happy to see me."

The man walked around in front of Haskell and pointed the gun at his chest. "I said, have a seat."

Haskell lowered himself to the ground, keeping his eye trained on Overton's trigger finger. Anger at his own stupidity nearly overrode his good sense.

Overton waved the gun. "Take off the vest."

Haskell's hand went automatically to the pocketed watch.

"Now."

He shrugged off the vest and held it on the tips of his fingers, ready to drop when Overton reached for it.

The man smirked. "Toss it to me."

Haskell ground his teeth and tossed the vest. Overton bent to retrieve it with his eyes and gun steady on Haskell.

Martha stepped away from the horse and snapped a twig.

"Stay right there, Marti, darlin', unless you want me blowin' a hole in Ranger Tillman here."

She stilled without a sound, her face cold, her eyes focused. *Not again for her, Lord, please. Not another killing.*

Overton put on the vest, felt in the pockets and pulled out the gold watch. "Nice timepiece ya got here, Tillman." A guttural laugh passed his lips. "I guess I should say *I* got here."

The smirk broadened as he dropped the watch in the pocket and tugged at the oversize vest.

"Marti, got any rope in that wagon?"

"No." She raised her chin and crossed her arms at her waist.

"Then tear off the bottom of that pretty little petticoat you're wearing and bring it over here nice and slow like."

Haskell fisted his hands and leaned forward.

"Don't even think about it, Tillman." The gun raised to Haskell's face. "I'm not above killin' ya right here among all the ripe fruit."

"You don't want a poster with your name on it for murder, Overton. Stop now and come back with me, and you'll just be tried for stealing horses."

Overton hacked out a sharp laugh and shook his head. "You're right funny, Tillman. What makes you think I'm stealin' horses?" He stepped back at an angle that put both of them in his line of vision. "Hurry up with that petticoat. We don't got all day."

Martha turned her back and lifted her skirt. The tearing sound ripped Haskell's heart open and all his regret and anger spilled out in a bitter gall.

Lord, please. You listened once, please hear me now and help me keep this man from harming the woman I love.

Chapter 17

Fear screamed in Martha's head, but she'd not give Tad Overton the satisfaction of hearing it.

Grasping the seam in her petticoat, she ripped it open, tearing away the bottom three inches and shredding her nerves. Birdsong mocked from the trees. Overly ripe apples vexed her nose, and a breeze tangled loose hair across her cheeks.

"Good girl." Tad waved the gun barrel toward Haskell. "Now tie his hands. Good and tight, mind you. You don't want me shootin' him 'cause he got loose and followed us, now do ya?"

She gripped the torn cloth with fisted fury. His voice repulsed her, and his arrogance stoked a fire fit to scorch the orchard, were she able to loose it. How had she ever found anything appealing or attractive about Tad Overton?

And how could she help Haskell now, here?

He held his hands out, crossed at the wrists. Overton cackled.

"Nice try, Tillman." The gun fanned the air. "Behind your back." He straightened his arm, aimed at Haskell's heart and steeled his voice to a deathly quiet. "You think I'm stupid?"

Don't answer. Don't answer. Please, Haskell, don't speak your mind, just this once. Martha knelt behind him and bound his hands with the eyelet-edged strip. Never had she dreamed the delicate trim would find such purpose as this.

She laid a hand on his shoulder and squeezed as she pushed herself up.

"Get away from him!"

She hurried sideways, toward the mare, and clawed through her mind for a way to stop Tad, free Haskell and escape.

Overton pulled off his neckerchief and dropped it. Then he drew a small vial from his trousers' pocket, pulled out the cork with his teeth and quickly turned his head. Stooping, he emptied the contents onto the neckerchief. Even at a distance, the pungent odor wrinkled her nose. *Chloroform.*

Panic filled her throat. He'd stolen the drug from Doc Mason and she doubted he knew its potency. Fully expecting him to use it on her, she gasped as Tad picked up the neckerchief and walked to Haskell.

With a sickening grin he circled behind his victim and reached around, covering Haskell's mouth and nose with the soaked cloth.

Tears fell involuntarily as Martha watched Haskell's weakening struggle. Finally, he slumped sideways. Tad knelt and held the rag against his face again.

"Stop it! You'll kill him!" She started forward and the gun quickly pointed her way.

"Not to worry. He's a big boy. Look at him." Overton grinned down at his helpless target. He laughed—the harsh, cold bark of a feral dog. "If a little is good, more is better, right?"

Martha bit her hand to keep from screaming.

Overton stuffed the rag in his back pocket, picked up Haskell's hat and shoved it on his own head with a smirk. "Not so tough, are you now, Ranger Tillman?" He landed a stiff boot against Haskell's back and walked to the wagon.

Martha shook with rage. God forgive her, but if she had

a gun she'd gladly shoot Tad Overton where he stood. She gripped her hands to steady them.

"Push those baskets out o' the wagon." The gun raked the air.

"No."

Without taking his eyes from her, Overton pointed the gun at Haskell's head. "What was that?"

With her jaw clamped so tight she feared she'd faint, Martha climbed to the seat and into the bed. One by one, she shoved the baskets off the opened end. They smashed onto the ground, bursting apart like Martha's memories of the day with Haskell. Apples bounced and rolled, and all their hard work, all their laughter and joy spilled across the grass and dirt until the wagon was empty and dry as her throat.

"That-a-girl. We don't need that extra weight holdin' us back."

She straightened and glared at him, her fingers balled into trembling fists. "I'll never be a part of your *we,* Tad Overton."

His laughter stilled the birds and scratched Martha's ears like little-boy nails across a chalkboard. "Take a seat, darlin'."

He climbed in beside her and scooted close as he reached over her lap for the reins. "Now ain't this cozy. Just like old times."

Remorse flooded her veins as his odor flooded her nostrils. If she hadn't fallen for his charms years ago, Haskell would not be lying in a heap in the orchard, his wrists bound and God knew how close to death. She glanced his way and tears filled her eyes. *Please, Lord, have mercy.*

With a loud *yah!,* Tad slapped the reins hard against Dolly and she lunged forward, startled by such abuse.

Martha jerked back and gripped the end of the seat with her right hand. "Where are we going?"

"Why, the Pueblo train depot, of course." The wagon rumbled down the narrow lane between the trees. Tad slowed little as they neared the barn. He pulled the hat low, laid his gun across his lap and shoved the barrel into her thigh. "You tell old man Blanchard thank you and smile real pretty when we go by, ya' hear? Don't make no signs if you plan on walkin' again anytime soon."

Martha's last hope of escape melted at the end of Tad's revolver.

Blanchard must have heard the wagon coming, for he stood at his barn entrance leaning on a pitchfork. Martha waved and raised her voice.

"Thank you, Papa Blanchard."

Tad glared at her and cocked the hammer. She glared right back as if she always called the church treasurer by such a familiar name. Lord help the man pick up on her hint. "See you Sunday."

She hoped.

Tad nearly lost control of the wagon at the turn and she rocked against his shoulder. When she looked back, Blanchard was trotting after them.

"What about my ladder?" Winded, he stopped and stood scratching his head as if he'd just seen a peculiar sight. She prayed he had and would do something about it.

At the main road, the wagon wheels skittered in a hard left turn. She had to leave a sign—anything for someone to follow. Something like the breadcrumbs from the storybook tale of two frightened children. But she couldn't reach the picnic basket in the back, and wagon wheels left no footprints. They would merely blend in with every other horse and wheel that traveled the hard-packed dirt to Pueblo.

Frantic to drop something, she bent over and fumbled with her boot laces. Tad said nothing and continued to drive the mare hard. Her mother's hat had fallen to the wagon floor and she eased it up and over the edge praying Tad wouldn't notice the flutter.

Another *yah!* and Dolly lunged again. Soaplike lather clung to her neck and sides where the harness rubbed. She'd never keep up the pace. Swallowing the guilt, Martha dared to pray the poor horse gave out *before* they reached the depot. Otherwise, there might be no chance of escape once they boarded the train out of town.

Haskell winced as he rolled to his back, crushing his bound hands beneath his weight.

Bound?

He blinked and squinted into leafy branches, trying to remember where he was and why.

Martha. Her fear-filled eyes.

He jerked up and the orchard spun, forcing him to his back. She was in danger. Of that he was certain, but nearly everything else was a blur. Everything except Tad Overton's mocking laughter.

He eased up and pulled at the cloth binding his hands, but it held fast. Heaving himself to his feet, he waited for the spinning to stop, then stumbled toward a rough-barked tree. The cloth quickly tore and he jerked free. Rubbing his wrists, he walked in widening circles until he found his gun. He spun the cylinder—six cartridges remained. Overton hadn't thought to unload it.

Anger warred with objectivity and he steeled himself against the rising emotion. He'd promised Martha he'd protect her and then he let a sniveling thief get the jump on them. Rage was a formidable enemy if allowed to overtake him. He needed hard, cold detachment to get Martha back, and he trained all his thoughts on that one purpose.

Holstering the Colt, he gathered his bearings and walked toward the lane. His pulse pounded at the sight of their morning's labor strewn across the ground—bushel baskets smashed in their heavy fall from the wagon and fruit scattered and damaged.

Forcing himself to breathe through his nose, he walked steadily in the direction of the barn, and by the time he arrived he was in a full trot. He needed a horse and he'd take one at the business end of his gun, if necessary. His badge lay in a hidden pocket in his vest. Another blunder.

"Blanchard," he hollered, approaching the barn. The man ran out leading a saddled horse with one hand holding a shotgun in the other.

The long double barrels raised. "Who are you?"

"I'm Haskell Jacobs, Colorado Ranger. I was wearing a hat and vest when you gave me the ladder."

Blanchard's ruddy face went white. "I knew something wasn't right."

The shotgun dipped, but the glare held steady. "Then who was that with Miss Marti?"

"That was the man I'm tracking, Tad Overton, in my vest and hat." Another step. "I need your horse to go after them."

Blanchard gave him the once-over. "How do I know you're really a ranger?"

"If my badge weren't in my vest, I could prove it. You're going to have to take my word."

Blanchard rubbed his chin, still holding the reins. Haskell's palms began to sweat. Time seeped by, stealing Martha farther away. He lowered his hands and rested one on the butt of his gun. "I need your horse, Blanchard. They're getting away—and I don't know which way they went."

Blanchard's eyes flicked to Haskell's gun hand. "I should have stopped them when they shot through the yard here without returning my ladder." He handed the reins to Haskell, stepped back and cradled the shotgun in his arm.

"I was gonna ride into town and see if Miss Marti was all right." He shook his head and stared down the lane.

Haskell swung into the saddle, itching to dig his boots into the bay's side and run for the wind. "Why do you say that?"

"She called me Papa Blanchard when they flew by." He looked at Haskell. "Why would she say that when we're no relation?"

Lightning fired through Haskell's skin and his fingers tightened to iron on the reins. The bay pranced, picking up its rider's agitation. "If you have another horse, I advise you ride in like you planned and tell Pastor Hutton and the sheriff. I doubt Overton'll go in on the main road. And he may have headed for Pueblo or Raton or God knows where."

Yes, God knows where.

Blanchard raised his hand. "You best be goin'. I'll let them know what's happening and send a telegram on to Pueblo just in case."

"I'm much obliged." The spirited bay reared under Haskell's tight hand. "I'll get your horse back to you."

"He's a good one. Dodger, I call him, 'cause he can dodge a prairie-dog hole before you know it's there."

Haskell leaned forward and rubbed the bay's neck, already slick beneath the reins. With a flick of his wrist, he whirled the horse around and it charged down the lane to the main road.

God, You know where they are. Please, show me. Help me find Martha. Keep her safe.

Haskell had prayed more in the last few days than in the ten years since his father took sick. And he prayed he'd get a different answer this time than he did to those long-ago prayers that failed to keep his father alive.

At the crossroad, he reined in and looked both ways. The nearest depot other than Cañon City was Pueblo. Overton wasn't known there. He could catch a train south to Raton or north to Denver. Or he could go east.

From the valley floor, Haskell saw only orchards, fields and distant mountains—a poor vantage point.

"Which way, Lord? I need Your help like I've never needed it before."

The bay swiveled its ears at his voice and pranced in a full circle. Haskell followed what he'd always thought was his gut and heeled the horse left toward Pueblo.

With the sun at his back, he chased his shadow. Just as he'd chased Tad Overton—always pursuing, never catching. But this time he pursued much more than a thief.

Something in the road ahead caught his attention and he pulled up.

The bay danced around it, its ears and nostrils strained at the wheel-flattened straw hat. Martha's hat. Did she throw it out on purpose or was she hurt?

His heart lurched and he flexed his fingers against their steely grip. "Steady, boy, steady." He rubbed the horse's lathered neck but the words were for himself. His father's words.

The hat was evidence that they'd ridden this way—not evidence that Martha was hurt. *Don't give your anger free rein. Steady. Hold steady.*

Leaning over Dodger's neck, he dug in his heels and the horse stretched into a dead gallop. The wind whipped the sweat from Haskell's face as soon as it formed and blew dust and grit in his eyes. He pushed on the reins, giving the horse its head, counting on Blanchard's confidence that the animal could dodge a chuck hole if need be.

The road crested a small rise and in the arroyo below the Huttons' wagon raised dust as the old mare kept to a frantic pace.

Joy leapt from Haskell's heart to his throat on its way

to a shout. But celebration was premature. He had to reach them first.

"Catch them, boy." The wind tore the words from his lips but their urgency telegraphed into Dodger's straining muscles. As if the bay knew, it charged into the dip and up the other side. With the heavy pull, the mare had slowed on the upward climb. Haskell was gaining on them.

A loud pop and hot air brushed his cheek. He ducked. Another bullet whizzed by.

Two shots. Four left. Haskell reached for his Colt. A few more yards and he'd be close enough to fire.

And close enough to hit Martha if the wagon veered. He holstered the gun and squinted into the wind. She didn't look back. She wasn't sitting straight, but was slumped against Tad.

He'd chloroformed her.

Haskell slapped leather against his mount. His spurs were at the hotel, not needed for a peaceful wagon ride to an apple orchard. Another mistake. He knew better than not to be prepared. Never again.

Another pop and heat grazed his ear. He flinched and jerked the reins left. Dodger swerved and Haskell quickly pulled him back to center. Another crest and the wagon disappeared over the top, picking up speed.

But the mare was fading. As Dodger chewed up the distance, curses shot past Haskell like bullets. When a wagon's length yawned between the buckboard and the bay's head, he kicked free of the stirrups.

Just a few more strides. Keep it up, boy, a little closer...

Haskell flung himself into the wagon. Overton swung his gun hand back as the wagon hit a rut and his bullet fell short, biting wood from the bed.

Two shots left.

Overton shoved the gun against Marti's chest and screamed. "Jump out or I'll kill her."

Haskell leapt over the seat, knocking the gun forward. The bullet shot past the mare's head, frightening her into a death race.

Haskell twisted the gun from Overton's hand and threw it out of the wagon. Then a fisted right hook sent the man over the back of the bench seat. Overton fell unconscious into the wagon bed.

The mare flattened her ears against her skull and her head bobbed with her efforts. Globs of white sweat flew back off her lathered hide.

Haskell snatched the reins with one hand and reached for Martha with the other. She slumped forward onto her knees and bounced against the end of the bench. One misstep by the faltering mare, and she could be thrown out.

He looped his right arm around Martha's waist and pressed her limp body against him as he reined in the mare. She slowed to a painful lope, then a trot, and he pulled her to a walk at the road's edge. Her sides heaved, her head hung and her forelegs buckled. She went down and the wagon jerked to a standstill.

Haskell turned Martha to face him and cradled her lolling head. Enfolding her in his arms, he rocked back and forth as he prayed, frantic that he'd reached her too late.

"God, please. Don't let me lose her."

His vision blurred as he drank in her pale features and smoothed her hair from her face.

"Don't leave me, Martha," he whispered. "I love you. Marry me. Be my wife and fill our home with your beauty and laughter and love." His voice broke on the last word and he crushed her limp body against him.

Chapter 18

Hoofbeats of pain pounded through Martha's head. Her face rubbed against a sweat-drenched shirt, a strong heart pulsing behind it. Steady, masculine, comforting. Haskell?

She pushed against the hard chest and looked up. The sun backlit the man and her eyes squinted against the light. But the smell, the tenderness, the substance of him said Haskell.

She breathed his name and felt a moan at her ear. The arms that encircled her set her upright. Rough hands cupped her face on each side. She blinked, trying to see, and raised a hand to shield the sun.

"Haskell?"

"Thank God." His voice choked and again his arms tightened around her. The throbbing in her head lessened and she surrendered to his embrace.

Reluctant to leave his comfort, she scooted back to sit on her own. Without the sun in her eyes, she clearly saw the tear trails on his dirty face, the shining, sky-filled eyes and blood atop his right ear. "You're hurt." She ran her fingers through his wind-whipped hair and laid a hand on his cheek.

"Just grazed. I'll heal."

"Oh, Haskell. I was so afraid he'd killed you."

He pulled her to him and pressed his lips against her forehead. "I'm sorry I didn't protect you."

"But you did."

He held her at arm's length and searched her face.

"You showed me how to leave a sign, a trail to follow." He laughed and kissed her forehead again.

"You saw it, didn't you? You saw my hat?"

A smile broke white in his dirty face. "I'll make a ranger of you yet."

She sniffed and straightened. "I should hope not. One rough ride like this is entirely enough for me."

A groan from the wagon bed jerked their heads in unison.

"Give me your boot laces," Haskell said as he climbed over the bench.

Martha untied her boots, stripped the long black laces and handed them to Haskell, who straddled Tad facedown on the wagon's floorboards. He pulled the vest from Tad's back and bound his hands. Then he pulled off the boots and bound his ankles.

Haskell grabbed his hat and returned to the bench seat where he slipped on the vest and felt the pockets. He drew out a gold fob anchored by a beautiful watch with scroll-work engraving the case in a fine *TJ*.

Martha laid her hand on his arm. "Where is the *H?*"

"There is no *H*. This was my father's watch—Tillman Jacobs. A Jefferson Ranger. He gave it to me the day he died. Someday I'll give it to my son."

Her heart clenched. How could she stand in the way of what he really wanted? She wrapped her arms around her middle to keep from breaking in half. "I'm so glad you got it back."

He returned it to the pocket and searched the vest's lining. Halting with discovery, he withdrew the ranger's star and pinned it to the front of his vest. "Blanchard wants proof I'm who I say I am when I take his horse back."

At that, he looked to Dolly who lay awkwardly in front

of the wagon. Martha had been so woozy she hadn't noticed that the poor thing had fallen in the harness.

Haskell helped Martha from the wagon and together
they stripped away the rigging.

She knelt at the mare's head and stroked her sweat-
soaked neck. "You poor thing," she whispered. "You dear,
faithful thing."

The smooth slide of steel against leather turned her head
and she looked up as Haskell cocked his gun.

He reached for her. "Stand behind me. You don't need
to see this."

"No. Please, no. Can't we help her in some way?" Fresh
tears squeezed up from Martha's soul, bitter with regret
for having prayed for the animal's demise.

Steel-etched eyes and a stern jaw met her pleading.
"What would you have me do? Leave her here to be eaten
alive by coyotes and buzzards?"

Martha gripped his arm. "We can get her up, get her
standing. Oh, Haskell, please. I know she may not make
it, but not now. Not like this." She covered her mouth with
both hands to hold back the sob.

He looked down at his boots, shook his head and eased
the hammer back. He holstered his gun, and together they
pulled the winded mare to her feet. Haskell set the brake
and tied her off to the front wheel.

"Thank you." Martha rested her forehead against his
chest and looped her arms around him. He stroked her hair
and in a low voice thanked the Lord for the mare's faithful heart and service.

Martha palmed the tears from her face and stepped
back. "Amen."

A whinny floated to them on the cooling breeze and
Martha looked east. A beautiful bay stallion stood next to
the road, head high, reins still around its neck.

Haskell whistled and the bay flicked his ears and tossed

his head. As if making clear the decision was his, he turned toward them and trotted to the wagon.

"Dodger." Haskell held his hand out as the horse approached and greeted them with a deep rumble.

"You're definitely a runner." He slipped the reins off and dropped them to the ground, then he hooked a stirrup on the saddle horn, checked the cinch and started to shorten the strap.

Martha stopped him. "Not this time, Haskell Jacobs." She pulled the stirrup down and patted it against the horse's side. "You're not walking back to town. You're riding. We're *both* riding."

His slow smile swirled through her.

"Don't look down," she said.

Her request doused the heat in his eyes and his brows raised in question.

"Better yet, close your eyes."

She lifted her skirt and wiped the dirt from his face. His eyelids fluttered.

"No peeking."

He gripped her wrist and his eyes flew open—two fiery blue gems in a sea of sweat and grit. "A bit forward, don't you think, Miss Hutton?"

"Not at all, Mr. Jacobs. I can't have my apple-picking escort looking like we chased halfway across Colorado."

Curses flew from the back of the wagon. Martha turned away abruptly, yanked at her petticoat and tore off a wide strip. "It's ruined anyway. We might as well do something constructive with what's left." She stuffed the fabric in Haskell's hands. "Do you mind?"

He jerked his nod. "With pleasure."

Haskell gagged their captive and left him flopping like a trout in the wagon bed.

"I recommend you stay facedown or the buzzards'll gouge your eyes out before the sheriff gets here."

At that, the flopping ceased, but not the guttural noises Martha equated with ungentlemanly expressions of wrath.

Haskell gathered the bay's reins, swung into the saddle and held out his hand. "Grab my wrist and I'll pull you up."

She complied and landed behind him astride the saddle's apron. Wrapping her arms around him, she laid her head against his broad back and they turned toward the sunset and home.

Grief puddled in her heart like a bitter rain. She had come so close to finding what she'd lost.

The dust cloud at the top of the first rise had to be the sheriff, Pastor Hutton or both. With daylight slipping behind the far ridgeline, Haskell couldn't make out the riders.

They met in the first arroyo he came to. Hutton rode up close and reached for Martha. "You're safe." His voice was thick with emotion. "Thank God, you're safe."

"Yes, Papa. Haskell got to us in time."

Hutton wiped his eyes and looked at Haskell. "Blanchard told us what happened. The sheriff telegraphed Pueblo and he should be along soon. He's got a few men riding with him." He looked up the road and back to Haskell.

"The wagon's behind us about two miles. Overton's tied in the bed."

"With my boot laces."

Haskell bit back a grin at the pride in Martha's voice. He wasn't sure how her father would take such talk, but she pressed on.

"And that strip of white you'll find in his mouth—that's my petticoat."

Shock swept Hutton's features, but he held his tongue.

"Overton's gun is somewhere out in the cholla," Haskell said. "I didn't look to see where I tossed it."

"And Papa." The pride drained from Martha's voice. "Dolly's nearly done in. Tad drove her like a fiend."

Haskell softened his tone. "She ran her heart out and buckled where we stopped. I don't know that she can make it back to town."

Hutton rubbed the back of his neck. "Better her than the two of you." He reset his hat and gave Martha a sad smile. "She was a good horse. Helped bring your ma and me together."

"I know, Papa. She was the little yellow filly, wasn't she?"

"That she was." He reined away. "I'll ride on and hitch the wagon to my horse, see how Dolly's doing."

Haskell shifted in the saddle. "She's tied to the off-side wheel."

Hutton left and they continued on. In another mile, the sheriff and his posse reined up in a galloping dust cloud.

"Overton's in the wagon bed, trussed and ready for shipment, maybe three miles on." Haskell thumbed over his shoulder. "I'll testify against him to charges of kidnapping, assault and attempted murder. I also believe he's the horse thief I was trailing, but we'll need a confession unless we can find those horses."

The sheriff pulled his hat brim. "Said you were the man for the job, didn't I?"

The eager group rode off and Haskell headed Dodger toward the orchard. At the turn, the stallion tried to lope, but he kept a tight rein to make Martha's ride as easy as possible.

Light filled the farmhouse windows and two lanterns hung at the barn doors. Haskell threw his right leg over the bay's head and jumped to the ground, then turned to help Martha. With her hands on his shoulders, he pulled her to him, holding her close in the stillness.

"I've got you now," he whispered against her hair. "You're safe."

She wriggled against him. "Put me down, please."

With a quick squeeze and a chuckle, he set her on her feet. "I'll put you down, but I'm not letting you go."

A shadow swept her face and she averted her eyes and stepped back. She'd done it again—switched leads without so much as a stumble. What happened?

Blanchard came out of the house, his wife on his heels and three youngsters trailing behind.

"Lord be praised," he said, slapping Haskell on the back like a long-lost relative.

A little pigtailed girl peeked around her mother's skirts. "You really a ranger, mister?"

Blanchard pointed at Haskell's vest. "See that, Priscilla? That's a ranger's star. He's the real thing."

"Would you stay to supper?" Blanchard's wife asked.

Martha moved her way, lightly touching a youngster's hair. "Thank you, Sarah. You are so kind, but I expect Mama is beside herself with worry since we missed the evening service, and I hate to keep her waiting any longer."

The woman embraced Martha in a brief hug. "You're right, you know. She's near frantic, according to what Foster told me when he got back from town. But you two take our wagon home. The one there in the barn. The children and I gathered all your apples and loaded them in fresh bushel baskets for you."

Martha covered her mouth with her hand.

"Thank you, ma'am." Haskell tipped his hat. "That's mighty generous of you."

"Can't have all that good fruit go to waste," Blanchard said, putting an arm around his wife. "Not when Mrs. Hutton's apple butter is at stake."

Haskell envied the man for his family, but pushed such thoughts aside. "You've got a fine horse here, Blanchard. As good as you said, if not better."

The man's chest swelled. "Got him for a song, I did. About two years ago, down in Raton. Off some fella who said he was fast as sheet lightning and sure-footed as a dance-hall gal."

"Foster!" Mrs. Blanchard clapped her hands over Priscilla's ears.

Blanchard himself blushed and ducked his head. "Sorry, Miss Marti. His words, not mine."

Haskell swallowed a grin and headed for the barn. Blanchard hurried forward and took the reins. "I'll take care of him. You get Miss Marti and those apples home. I can get the other horse and the wagon when I come to town Sunday."

Haskell shook his head at the man's generosity. "Thank you, Blanchard. I'm much obliged."

The wagon held baskets filled to the brim. More than they'd started with, if Haskell's count was right, and a horse stood ready and harnessed. He extended his hand to Martha who came to his side with eyes downcast. His heart twisted. Something had sapped her joy and left her fragile and weak.

He helped her to the seat and settled beside her. With a flick of the reins, they drove out of the open barn, past the family and into the night. He ached to feel Martha's warm body against him, but she sat apart, straight and stoic.

If it were a man who had stolen her tenderness, he could fight him, defend her. But his foe was beyond the reach of his gun or his fists.

His gut told him words were the culprit, and words had never been his weapon of choice.

As helpless as a lost pup, he headed out of the valley and up the rise toward Cañon City.

Chapter 19

The evening star hung alone and bright in the paling sky, a single ornament strung above the mountain silhouette. Solitary, like Martha, though she sat inches from a man to whom she'd gladly give her heart and life. She breathed in the cooling air and her insides chilled. Brimming like the new bushel baskets behind them, she was bursting with love for this man who had risked his life for her. He was so much more than she could have ever hoped for.

And she was so much less than he needed or wanted.

Once he knew the truth, he'd not be so eager to marry her.

A shiver rippled up her back.

Haskell pulled her beneath his arm. "You cold?"

Frozen rigid. "A little."

Unable to resist his warmth, she tucked against his side.

"It won't be long. The lights of town are just ahead."

He squeezed her arm, pressing her closer. The gesture deepened the pain of what she would lose again—the love and warmth of a caring man.

As they drove into the quiet town, the horse's plodding hoofbeats echoed off closed storefronts. No light shone from the church, the service canceled with her father gone. But through the trees, the parsonage's glowing windows promised warmth and comfort. Haskell turned down their lane and drove into the open barn. Martha straightened and pushed at her hair, discovering more of it worked loose from her twisted braid than captured by it. She must look a sight.

He jumped down and stood beside the wagon with his hands lifted for her, his eyes dark and churning as she imagined the sea in a storm. Her heart reached for her throat as she reached for his shoulders, and he set her lightly on the ground.

Consuming her with his gaze, a question formed on his features. "Martha, you—"

"Oh, thank God." Her mother's voice broke with a sob as she hobbled into the barn, clutching a shawl around her shoulders. "Thank God you're safe."

He groaned and quickly kissed the top of Martha's head before stepping back.

Her mother's eyes were red with weeping. Martha palmed her cheek. "Don't cry, Mama. We're safe. The Lord took fine care of us."

Her mother squeezed Haskell's forearm, then tugged her shawl closer with one hand and drew Martha with the other. "The apples can wait. Come inside, get warm and have something to eat, both of you."

"I'll tend to the horse. You go ahead."

The remark drew her mother's notice and she threw a questioning look at Martha. "Where's Dolly?" A closer inspection of the green wagon raised her brows. "And our buckboard?"

"Dolly nearly died running her heart out, Mama, but let us tell you all about it inside." She turned from Haskell with as much detachment as she could summon. "Haskell spared her."

She understood his compassionate gesture to end Dolly's suffering, but she'd never have been able to tell her mother Haskell had shot the horse she'd raised from a filly, old though she was.

Enclosed in the barn, the wagon load of crisp, ripe fruit filled the air with a cidery promise.

"You certainly picked a lot today." Martha's mother pulled out several apples and tucked them in her shawl. "These will make a fine pie for tomorrow's dinner."

"We didn't pick them, Mama, but that's all part of the story. Come on."

By the time Haskell came in and washed for supper, they heard horses outside. Moments later, her father trudged in, dusty and tired from hard riding and harder worry. He held a hand out to Haskell and topped it with his other in a hardy grip. Then he pulled Martha into his arms. The breath caught in his chest and the sound pushed a knot to her throat.

Finally, he held her back with a loving smile. "Thank You, Lord, and thank you, Haskell."

Haskell's features sobered. "My pleasure, Pastor."

Martha kept her eyes from meeting his. She would refuse him, spare him the pain of retracting his proposal once he learned she could not give him what he longed for.

Oh, Lord, let me not bleed to death right here at the table.

They all took their seats and hands reached out to either side for prayer. Haskell's swallowed Martha's, as always, and he squeezed her fingers. Her heart split like an apple beneath a boot heel.

At the *Amen,* her father picked up his coffee and held it with both hands, elbows pitched on the table as if for support.

"Dolly's in the barn." His eyes latched onto his wife's. "She's in bad shape, Annie. I don't know if she'll make it through the night."

Her mother's face crumpled into a silent cry and she hid behind her hands.

He rubbed her shoulder. "She had a good life, sweetheart. You know that."

Her mother nodded and sniffed. Martha thanked God again that Haskell had not shot the old mare.

"And Tad Overton is behind bars."

At the news, Haskell's lips curled and he reached for the butter crock.

He had to be starving after all he'd been through. With a start, Martha remembered his ear and leaned forward to see it, catching uncertainty in his eyes. He'd sensed her withdrawal.

Grief surged through her like a fever. "Your ear. We should dress it."

Her parents looked at Haskell and he fingered the dried blood. "It's just a flesh wound."

"I didn't even notice, Mr. Jacobs." Her mother wiped her eyes with her napkin and drew in a broken breath. "I was so glad to see the both of you, I guess I didn't look any closer. What happened?"

"Tad shot him." Martha shuddered. "At least that's what I think happened. I didn't exactly see it."

Her mother's jaw went slack.

"Is that what happened?" Her father directed his question to Haskell.

"Yes, sir. Overton had Martha in the wagon. He'd chloroformed her and I was gaining on them while he was shooting."

"Chloroform? Shooting?" Her mother's voice hit a rare note and her face blanched.

Her father moved his chair closer to his wife and tucked her beneath his arm. "I think you'd better start from the beginning, son."

To hear the event retold from Haskell's perspective, he'd hardly lifted a finger. He failed to mention risking his life to save her. The more she listened, the more she loved this man so deserving of everything he dreamed of. She scooted from the table.

"Excuse me, but I'm exhausted." She faced Haskell but kept her eyes down. Maybe he would accept this parting as her refusal and be on his way. "Thank you for helping me today. I trust you'll have a safe journey to Denver with your prisoner."

Silence hung in the room like the evening star over the mountains. She laid her napkin in her plate and went to the parlor. Tired, yes. Tired enough to sleep, no. She'd lay on the settee, put her feet up, perhaps doze. There would be plenty of time to sleep later. Alone.

She closed the parlor doors behind her and her parents' voices blurred to concerned mumbles. She imagined them questioning Haskell about every detail.

His deep tones answered theirs and, at times, rose with a curious urgency. What could he be discussing at such length? Surely it was time for him to leave.

She placed a cushion beneath her neck as Haskell had that pivotal day he'd nearly trampled her in the street. The irony bit. As it turned out, he'd merely trampled her heart.

Her eyes closed against the darkness and the muted voices drifted beyond her ears.

Haskell pushed the parlor doors apart and the kitchen light spread across the room to Martha's sleeping form. He moved to her side and pulled the small stool beneath him as he had once before. Reaching for her hand, he took it in both of his, hoping, praying she'd not be frightened by his nearness, but would welcome it.

And he prayed for wisdom, for compassion. Not only had he missed the importance of her not having children, he had also misread her parents. They did not see him as a hired gun, not as far as Martha was concerned, but they did endorse his decision to return to Cañon City and run for sheriff.

After a trial in Cañon City, and if he could prove Overton was the horse thief, Haskell figured on a month to transport his prisoner, testify in Denver and make it back to Cañon. In that time, Pastor Hutton promised to look for a house Haskell could rent until he bought a place of his own in the country. A place of *their* own.

If she'd still have him.

"Martha." He whispered her name and brushed her cheek with the back of his hand. She turned her head and her eyelashes fluttered with a dream.

"Martha." He squeezed her hand. "Wake up. I need to ask you something before I leave."

She jerked and her eyes flew open, dark and wide in the dim light.

"It's me. Don't be frightened." He pressed his lips against her tightened fingers and helped her sit up.

"What happened? What's wrong?"

"Nothing is wrong. Everything is right. At least I hope so."

She pulled her hand away and buried it in her skirts. Her eyes glistened, and she looked ready to flee the room.

His conversation with her parents, and what he believed to be her genuine affection for him, steeled his will to continue. "I love you, Martha."

She blinked. Her lips parted, and a small gasp escaped.

"Marry me. Sit on my porch swing and share what's left of this old man's life."

Her lips trembled and her brow crushed together. "You are not an old man, Haskell Jacobs." She glanced down and rolled her lips. "But—" She peeked up at him. "In the orchard. I was not completely truthful with you."

He knew now, but he let her say it.

"I am not all that you think I am."

Clasping her hands tightly, she drew a deep breath. "There is something you should know about me that could change the way you feel."

A smile pulled at his mouth "I already know about your two last names."

She choked out a halfhearted laugh but shook her head. Then she raised that defiant chin he had come to love.

"You will have no son to give your father's watch if you marry me. Nor any daughters." Her eyes pooled and her voice fell to a whisper. "I am barren."

The groan broke deep in his chest and he pulled her into his arms. "My sweet Martha." Gladly he'd spend the rest of his life proving she was more than enough. "I don't need a son if I have you."

A shudder rippled through her.

"Your love means more to me than many sons or daughters."

She pushed free and held both hands to her mouth. Above them, dark eyes searched his face, hoping, doubting, pleading.

How to convince her? He couldn't lose her now, not because of her doubts, not after all they'd been through.

"Do you need proof?"

She blinked again and a jewel slipped from her eyes and down her face.

"What did your father say? The day of the basket social."

Her brows furrowed and she glanced away, remembering.

"If you cannot see the evidence of my love, then take it on faith."

She closed her eyes and shook her head. His insides knotted. Had he misjudged her feelings after all?

"Oh, Haskell." A wind whisper through the pines. He shivered at the sound.

"I have loved you with such hope."

He pulled her to him and her arms went round him with a quivering breath. Then he raised her chin and gently kissed the tears from her lips.

"Who knows what God has in store for us, Martha? He proved that to me the day I watched a red-haired beauty in black step from the train."

A breathy laugh pushed against his chest. "Only you would see beauty where there was nothing but pain." She sat back and brushed at her damp cheeks. "I suppose there is more than one way to fill a home with love and laughter."

"Who's to say there is not a child somewhere who needs the same? More than one, or a whole house full."

Her smile spilled over him, soothing all the old scars, healing every longing.

"A porch, you say?" She slanted a teasing glance.

His heart raced. "And a swing."

She held out her delicate hand in acceptance.

"Well, in that case, the answer is yes, Haskell Tillman Jacobs. I would love nothing more than to spend the rest of my life with you."

* * * * *

REQUEST YOUR FREE BOOKS!

2 FREE INSPIRATIONAL NOVELS
PLUS 2
FREE
MYSTERY GIFTS

Love Inspired

LIDIR13

REQUEST YOUR FREE BOOKS!

2 FREE INSPIRATIONAL NOVELS
PLUS 2
FREE
MYSTERY GIFTS

Love Inspired
HISTORICAL
INSPIRATIONAL HISTORICAL ROMANCE

YES! Please send me 2 FREE Love Inspired® Historical novels and my 2 FREE mystery gifts (gifts are worth about $10). After receiving them, if I don't wish to receive any more books, I can return the shipping statement marked "cancel." If I don't cancel, I will receive 4 brand-new novels every month and be billed just $4.74 per book in the U.S. or $5.24 per book in Canada. That's a savings of at least 21% off the cover price. It's quite a bargain! Shipping and handling is just 50¢ per book in the U.S. and 75¢ per book in Canada.* I understand that accepting the 2 free books and gifts places me under no obligation to buy anything. I can always return a shipment and cancel at any time. Even if I never buy another book, the two free books and gifts are mine to keep forever.

102/302 IDN F5CY

Name	(PLEASE PRINT)	
Address		Apt. #
City	State/Prov.	Zip/Postal Code

Signature (if under 18, a parent or guardian must sign)

Mail to the Harlequin® Reader Service:
IN U.S.A.: P.O. Box 1867, Buffalo, NY 14240-1867
IN CANADA: P.O. Box 609, Fort Erie, Ontario L2A 5X3

Want to try two free books from another series?
Call 1-800-873-8635 or visit www.ReaderService.com.

* Terms and prices subject to change without notice. Prices do not include applicable taxes. Sales tax applicable in N.Y. Canadian residents will be charged applicable taxes. Offer not valid in Quebec. This offer is limited to one order per household. Not valid for current subscribers to Love Inspired Historical books. All orders subject to credit approval. Credit or debit balances in a customer's account(s) may be offset by any other outstanding balance owed by or to the customer. Please allow 4 to 6 weeks for delivery. Offer available while quantities last.

Your Privacy—The Harlequin® Reader Service is committed to protecting your privacy. Our Privacy Policy is available online at www.ReaderService.com or upon request from the Harlequin Reader Service.

We make a portion of our mailing list available to reputable third parties that offer products we believe may interest you. If you prefer that we not exchange your name with third parties, or if you wish to clarify or modify your communication preferences, please visit us at www.ReaderService.com/consumerschoice or write to us at Harlequin Reader Service Preference Service, P.O. Box 9062, Buffalo, NY 14269. Include your complete name and address.

LIHDIR13R

ReaderService.com

Manage your account online!

- Review your order history
- Manage your payments
- Update your address

*We've designed
the Harlequin® Reader Service
website just for you.*

Enjoy all the features!

- Reader excerpts from any series
- Respond to mailings and
  special monthly offers
- Discover new series available to you
- Browse the Bonus Bucks catalog
- Share your feedback

Visit us at:
ReaderService.com

RS13